Underdog

Eric Walters

ORCA BOOK PUBLISHERS

National Library of Canada Cataloguing in Publication Data

Walters, Eric, 1957-
Underdog / Eric Walters.

(Orca young readers)
ISBN 1-55143-302-8

I. Title. II. Series.

PS8595.A594U53 2004   jC813'.54   C2004-901649-0

Library of Congress Control Number: 2004103572

Summary: The seventh installment in Eric Walters' popular basketball series for young readers.

Free teachers' guide available.

Orca Book Publishers gratefully acknowledges the support for its publishing programs provided by the following agencies: the Government of Canada through the Book Publishing Industry Development Program (BPIDP), the Canada Council for the Arts, and the British Columbia Arts Council.

Cover design by Lynn O'Rourke
Cover and interior illustrations by John Mantha

In Canada:	**In the United States:**
Orca Book Publishers	Orca Book Publishers
Box 5626, Stn.B	PO Box 468
Victoria, BC Canada	Custer, WA USA
V8R 6S4	98240-0468

07 06 05 04 • 6 5 4 3 2 1
Printed and bound in Canada
Printed on 100% post-consumer recycled paper,
100% old growth forest free, processed chlorine free
using vegetable, low VOC inks.

*For all those who know what it's like
to be an underdog—and still win!*
—E.W.

I

I threw up the shot. It hit the front of the rim and bounced harmlessly away.

"That's 'G'!" Kia yelled out.

"I know that," I said.

"And that means you lose, Nick," she said.

"I know that too."

"So, Mark wins...again."

"Big surprise," I said as I ran over and retrieved the ball before it could roll away down the street. "Mark always wins."

Mark gave a shy little smile. He'd won all five games of "pig" the three of us had played, but he'd never brag about it or anything. That just wasn't him. Actually, just talking wasn't him. He was about the quietest person in the world.

"I'm tired of playing pig anyway," Kia said.

"Me too," I agreed. Kia was my best friend. She'd been my best friend since we were really little, so I knew she didn't like losing any more than I did. And playing a game like pig with Mark was almost a guarantee of losing. He was impossible to beat in any game that involved simply shooting a basketball.

"How about if we play a little two-on-two?" Kia suggested.

"Maybe I can't beat Mark at pig, but at least I can count," I replied.

"And what is that supposed to mean?" Kia asked.

"Look around, Kia. Two-on-two basketball would involve two plus two players. If you haven't noticed, there are only three people standing here on the driveway," I said.

"Actually I'm pretty good at math. Three plus one equals four, so that means we only need one more player," she replied.

"And where do you think we're going to get that extra player? I've already called David and Jamie, Tristan, Paul and—"

"I'm not talking about calling anybody. How about that kid?" Kia said, pointing down the street to the little park.

"The kid on the swings?"

"Yeah."

A kid had slowly walked by on the other side of the street a couple of times while we were playing. As he'd walked by, he watched us play while he pretended not to watch us. None of us knew who he was, so that meant he didn't live around here. The kid was now sitting on a swing in the park a half dozen houses down from my house. He wasn't swinging, just sitting there.

"How do you know he even plays basketball?" I asked.

"I won't know until I ask him."

"You're just going to walk up to him and ask if he wants to play?" I asked.

"Unless you want to go."

"Not me!" I exclaimed and backed away a step.

"How about you, Mark?" she asked.

Mark just shook his head. Mark didn't even like to talk to people he knew, so I couldn't

3

imagine him walking up to a stranger and starting a conversation.

"Then it looks like it will be me."

Kia took the basketball from my hands and started off toward the park, dribbling the ball as she walked. Mark and I stood there just watching—after all, since she'd taken the ball, what choice did we have but to watch? She walked right up to the boy and it looked like she started talking—not that we were close enough to hear, but what else would she be doing?

"She's got a lot of guts," Mark said. "I'd never go up and talk to a stranger."

"You hardly talk to the people you do know."

Mark chuckled softly under his breath. My mother joked that she thought Mark was just waiting for a break in the conversation between Kia and me—a break that never did come. I loved having a mother who thought she was funny.

It was true that Kia and I did talk a lot, but there was a whole lot more that we didn't even need to say. We'd been best friends since around the time we'd learned to speak, and because of that we just knew what the other was thinking without even needing to put it in words.

The boy got off the swing and he and Kia started walking back. Actually she was walking and he was dribbling the ball. Even from the distance it was obvious that he could handle the ball. He did a little cross-over through his legs a couple of times, and the ball danced between his hands and the pavement. I watched them walk toward us.

The kid was a little taller than Kia. She was just about the tallest person in our grade, so he was at least a year older. He was wearing a football jersey, a big silver necklace dangling around his neck, baggy pants and a head-band. As he got closer I could tell that he also had a big shiny stud in one ear.

I'd once mentioned to my mother that I'd like to get an ear pierced. She said when I became a pirate I could get an earring...and a parrot to go along with it.

There was one other thing about the kid. He was black. Not that that made any differ-ence. He just was.

"This is Ashton," Kia said, "and these guys are Nick and Mark."

"Hi," I said.

"Pleased to meet you," Mark said.

He nodded his head in greeting.

"Ashton said he'll play some ball with us," Kia said. "The only question is what are the teams?"

"Who's the best of you three?" Ashton asked.

"We're all different but about the same," Kia replied. "We all play rep."

"Rep?"

"We play for the Mississauga Magic team. We represent this city when we play against the best players from other cities," she explained.

"We've been together for years," I added.

"If you say so," he said, but he didn't sound like he was impressed. "Tell you what," he said, looking at me. "Why don't you take whoever you want and I'll take the other one."

"No, you pick," I said.

"Nope, I think you should. Pick who ever's the best. That way it might be a game," he said.

7

Who did he think he was? Just because he had a crossover dribble and some jewelry didn't mean he could play ball.

"How about if I take the girl?" he said. "Just to make it more even."

"The girl's name is Kia, remember?" Kia snapped. "And I don't think I want to be on your team. I'd rather be on the winning side."

To my shock he started laughing. "Good one," he said. "Very good. You take Kia and I get the little guy." He tossed me the ball. "Shoot for possession."

I walked to the foul line. If I made the shot, we got the ball. If I missed, it was their ball to begin. I took a deep breath, bounced the ball exactly three times and spun it backward in my hands. This was my free throw routine. Always the same. Never different. At least not until I missed three shots in a row and then I'd change everything.

Bending at the knees, remembering to use my legs, I put up the shot. It swooshed!

"Our ball," Kia said. She grabbed the ball and we walked to the top of the key.

"Mark knows all our plays as well as we do so we have to work on Ashton. Let's work the pick-and-roll and try a lot of backdoor plays," she whispered. "I get the feeling he's going to jump out at things and try to steal the ball."

I nodded. "I'll in-bounds the ball."

Ashton came out and stood in front of me.

"Check," I said as I bounced him the ball and he tossed it back.

Kia ran free of Mark and I threw her the ball. Instantly I set up a pick, and as she broke around me to shake Mark off, Ashton rushed forward to block her. I spun around and was completely open. Kia tossed me a soft little lob pass that dropped right into my hands. I laid it in for an easy two points.

"That's the first points of the game," Kia cackled.

Ashton took the ball. "First points don't matter as much as the last points of the game. You know, the ones that win the game."

Ashton gave the ball to Mark. "You toss it in."

Mark checked the ball with Kia and then put in a perfect pass to Ashton. Ashton began dribbling. He faked me in and out, putting the ball back and forth between his legs from one hand to the other. He was good. I knew if I lunged forward he'd be able to break round me. I backed off a half step, hoping he wouldn't—or couldn't—shoot.

"You coming out to get me or what?" he asked.

"I think I'll wait right here."

Ashton suddenly broke for the net, faking to my right and trying to charge around the left. It was a good move, but I had the angle to seal him off and—he did a lightning fast behind-the-back move, broke around me and put in his own easy lay-up!

"That was some move," I gasped.

"You haven't seen anything yet," he said.

Kia and I walked to the top of the key. "You want me to cover him?" she asked quietly.

"You think you can do any better?"

"Couldn't do any worse than that," she replied.

"How about if you just move a little and give me some help," I whispered.

"If I double down he'll just kick it out to Mark for an open jumper."

"I don't think that'll happen," I said. "Didn't you notice the way he dribbles?"

"You mean the way he broke you off at the ankles?"

"Funny. No, the way he didn't even look at Mark. Let's see if he even notices the open man."

"Are you two playing or praying?" Ashton yelled at us.

"I'll throw it in," I said to Kia. I checked the ball with Ashton and instantly threw a strike to Kia. She turned toward the hoop but was immediately double teamed. Kia kicked it back out to me and I had another clear lane to the basket. I drove in and—"Ouch!" I screamed as Ashton bowled me over and I fell to the ground.

"Foul!" Kia screamed.

"Hard foul!" I added.

Ashton offered me a hand and helped pull me to my feet. "I couldn't let you go clean to the net. Besides, there's no point in fouling unless you foul hard."

11

"That's what our coach always says," Kia added.

"Then you got a smart coach," Ashton said. "You get two foul shots."

"Next basket is game for us," Kia announced as she handed the ball to Ashton.

He grumbled out something under his breath. While I couldn't understand the words, I knew the attitude. He was not happy about how things were going. Then again, I wouldn't be happy if my team was losing thirteen to six.

Of course, it was wrong to say his team was losing because he really didn't have a team. Other than putting the ball into play, Mark had hardly handled the ball. As soon as it got into Ashton's hands it was gone. He dribbled and drove and dipsy-doodled and then shot.

If I'd have been Mark I would have been yelling for the ball, but that wasn't Mark. He just stood there, quiet, waiting for the ball.

It had gotten to the point where Kia was hardly bothering to cover Mark anymore.

What was the point? Despite Mark being completely open, Ashton never kicked the ball back to him. That was lucky because it did take the two of us to cover him, and if he did get the ball to Mark, there was no way Mark would miss a shot that was that open.

This kid could really dribble. But I didn't know much about the rest of his game. I certainly didn't know how well he could pass—actually I didn't even know if he could pass. And I didn't know anything about his outside shooting. All he did was dribble and drive, but boy could he do those things.

Once again Mark in-bounded the ball to Ashton. He immediately began a series of wild moves. I'd learned to stay back off him a couple of feet. If you tried to close in he'd make you look bad. But since he didn't shoot it was okay to play off a step or even two. His whole game was beating his man and driving to the net. Once I knew that, stopping him wasn't that hard—well, at least it wasn't impossible. Then again, if Kia wasn't helping me out, he might have still been able to get around me.

With both Kia and me blocking him, there was no way he was going to get by us, but that wasn't going to stop him from trying. He tried to drive between us. Kia reached out and poked the ball away. It bounced to Mark. He set and then put up a shot. It swooshed right in.

"Nice shot!" Ashton yelled. Mark smiled ever so slightly and shrugged.

Kia took the ball and checked it with Mark.

"He can make those shots all day," Kia said. "Not that it matters now because the game is over."

"It's not over!" Ashton protested.

"No, you're wrong, it's over," Kia said.

"All we have to do is make the next three baskets and—"

Kia lobbed in a high pass over Ashton and Mark. While they'd been arguing I'd faded in behind them and was completely open under the net. I grabbed the pass and put in a very easy, unopposed lay-up.

"You were saying?" Kia asked.

2

"So we gonna play again?" Ashton asked.

"Why not?" Kia replied. "Sometimes we play until it gets dark."

"In my neighborhood they sometimes play until it gets light," Ashton said.

"What does that mean?" I asked.

"It means that they play ball all night long. If I leave my bedroom window open, I can hear the sound of the bouncing ball all the way up to the twenty-seventh floor."

"That's pretty high up," I said.

"Yeah. It's really high."

"It must be some view," Kia added.

"It is. If you stand on the railing of the balcony you can see all the way downtown."

"You stand on the railing of your balcony on the twenty-seventh floor?" I gasped. I hated heights. No, that was wrong. I didn't just hate heights, I was terrified of them.

"Not me. One of my brothers does."

"He just stands up on the railing?" I asked, not able to believe that anybody would do that.

"Don't you try to stop him?" Kia asked.

"He's my big brother. I can't stop him from doing anything. Besides, it's not like he does it all the time. It was just a couple of times. It made my stomach do a flip watching him."

"It makes my stomach flip just hearing you tell me about watching him," I said.

"So are we going to play again or what?" Ashton asked.

"Sure, do you want to go with the same teams or—"

"Heellloooo!" My mother's voice came floating out of the house. "Muffins are out of the oven!"

"So much for playing!" Kia said. "Time for a snack!"

Kia and Mark headed for the front door.

"Okay...thanks for the game," Ashton said as he took the ball and rolled it onto the grass.

"Don't you want to play anymore?" I asked.

"Yeah, but you're stopping."

"We'll play after we take a break...you do like muffins, don't you?" I asked.

"Um...yeah...I guess," he stammered.

"Then come on."

"Are you sure that's okay?" he asked.

"Why wouldn't it be? You think she only baked three muffins?"

Ashton laughed. "It's not that...It's just that...you know...your mother might not want you to bring a stranger into the house."

"Stranger? Your name is Ashton, isn't it?"

"Of course it is."

"Then you're not a stranger. But we better get inside fast. We've given Mark and Kia too much of a head start. There might not be any muffins left by the time we get there."

Ashton followed me into the house. I kicked off my shoes and he did the same. I led him down the hall and into the kitchen. Kia and

Mark were already sitting at the table, a partially drunk glass of milk and an empty muffin wrapper in front of each of them. They were already working on seconds.

"Are there any left, you pigs?" I asked.

Kia started oinking and Mark chuckled.

"Don't worry, I baked three dozen," my mother said. Her back was to us.

"Mom, I'd like you to meet somebody," I said.

She turned around and gave Ashton a big smile.

"Mom, this is Ashton."

He rushed over and held out his hand to shake. "Pleased to meet you, ma'am."

"You have wonderful manners," my mother said, and I thought how he didn't greet any of us that way.

"Thank you, ma'am," he said. "My mother always insists that me and my brothers formally address adults."

"Now, you and Nick wash your hands and I'll have a nice big glass of milk and a muffin—"

"A muffin?" I asked, cutting her off.

"Okay, a few muffins waiting for you."

I hurried over to the kitchen sink with Ashton in tow.

"Those muffins really smell fantastic, ma'am," he said as he began to wash his hands.

"Thank you. And they taste even better than they smell. Right, Kia...right, Mark?"

They both mumbled out agreement through a mouthful of muffin.

"So, Ashton, do you go to school with Kia and Nick?" my mother asked.

"No, ma'am. I go to Brookmeade."

"Brookmeade? That's not even close to here," she said.

"It's no farther than Mark's school," I said. Kia and I went to the same school, but Mark's school was halfway across the city.

"If you don't go to school together, how did you get to know these kids?" she asked.

"Playing basketball," I said, answering for him. "You know how it is. Every kid who plays ball is a friend with every other kid." For some reason I didn't want her to know that we'd just met twenty minutes ago.

"I see," she said. She had that look like she was getting ready to think of her next question. It wasn't that my mom was nosy, but she was a reporter for the local paper and liked asking questions. Actually, come to think of it, she was a reporter, but she also was sort of nosy. She always knew everybody and everything about their lives.

"And you should see Ashton play," Kia added.

"He's got incredible ball skills," I agreed.

"Better than you three?" my mother asked.

"He's got some great moves," I said.

"Then maybe he should try out for your team," she suggested.

"He's too old," I said.

"Too old?" my mother questioned. "But doesn't Brookmeade only go to grade five?"

"Yeah," Ashton said. "I'm in grade five."

"You are?" I asked in astonishment. "Are you supposed to be in grade five?"

"What do you mean by that?" he asked. He sounded irritated.

"It's just that you're pretty big," I said. "I just thought that because you're so big that maybe...maybe... "

"That maybe I failed a grade?" he asked.

20

I nodded.

"I'm exactly where I'm supposed to be," he said. "I've never failed anything in school, ever."

"I didn't mean anything bad," I said. "It's just that you're bigger than anybody in our whole school who's in grade five."

"What grade are you three in?"

"We're all in grade five," Kia said.

"And you're all supposed to be in grade five?" he asked.

"Of course we're supposed to be in grade five," she answered.

"Then you're all in the same grade and the same age, so Ashton could try out for your team," my mother said.

"He could," I said.

"We even have a couple of openings," Kia said. "We could really use an extra point guard."

Mark nodded in agreement.

"The tryouts are on Saturday," Kia added. "One to three o'clock at Sheridan College, main gym."

"There'll be lots of kids, but you're a really good player," I said. "We could even tell Coach about you, so it wouldn't be like you were a stranger to him."

"Are you interested in coming out?" Kia asked.

Ashton shrugged. "I might be. I only have one question."

"What's that?" I asked.

He turned to my mother. "Do you think I could have another muffin, ma'am?"

3

"Come on, boys and girl, it's time for a little basketball!" Coach Barkley yelled. "Everybody, let's have five laps to get warmed up!"

We started jogging around the perimeter of the gym.

"How many people you figure are here?" I asked Kia as we rounded a corner.

"Maybe sixty, but don't worry, you'll make the team"

"I'm not worried about that...not much. I was just wondering, that's all."

"Pick it up!" Coach yelled and we kicked it up a notch.

"He's not here," Kia said.

I ran a quick mental list. Everybody from last year's team was here. "Who's not here?"

"Ashton."

"Oh, yeah. Did you really think he was going to come?" I asked.

"I didn't know, but I figured he might want to— "

"Nick! Kia! Did you two come out here to play basketball or have a little chat? 'Cause I wouldn't want this tryout to get in the way of your socializing!"

We both put our heads down and started running a little bit harder. This was a new record. I didn't think anybody had annoyed Coach this early in a tryout or practice. And annoying Coach Barkley was not a good idea.

We completed the fifth lap and came to a stop. A couple of kids—kids who didn't know Coach—went to get their water bottles from the bleachers. Those of us who knew him knew this was a mistake. A big mistake. *A really big mistake.*

"Anybody who needs a drink and a break can take one!" Coach bellowed. "In fact, they

24

can take a break for the next few months because they won't be on my team!"

The couple of guys who had grabbed water bottles dropped them and rushed back out to join us.

"Nick," Coach said, and I felt a little jolt of electricity go up my spine. Was he going to say something else about Kia and me talking or that I hadn't run fast enough or..."Go into the middle and lead everybody in some stretchcs," Coach said.

Kia walked over with me to the center of the gym. "You really are Coach's pet, aren't you? Hey, there's Ashton!"

Ashton had just come in through the double doors at the end of the gym. He put down his bag and rushed over and joined everybody else as they started to form a big circle around me. I wondered if Coach noticed him coming in late.

"Just so people know!" Coach yelled. "There's probably nothing I hate as much as late." Obviously he had noticed Ashton's entrance. "For the next tryout, if you come late, don't even bother coming at all!"

Coach was in a fine mood. I'd start the stretches and try to keep out of his way.

"That's it!" Coach called out. "Everybody gather around!"

I joined the group of players assembling around Coach. It was certainly a much smaller group than had started the tryout two hours before. Coach had gone around and told a bunch of kids that they weren't going to make the team, and they'd already left. I knew that was hard, but it was pretty obvious to me that some kids were way out of their league here, and there was no point in wasting time, pretending they could play rep ball.

"Congratulations," Coach said. "The people who are still in the gym have made the first cut. You're all invited to come back next week."

That felt good. Not that I thought I was in any danger of getting cut in the first round, but it still felt good.

"I'm pleased with what I've seen today," Coach continued. "Good hustle, good skills, some real good ball handling."

Coach glanced over to where Ashton stood. I knew he was referring to him. Ashton had been showing off his stuff, and there was nobody who could handle him one on one. He had really impressed people, and a couple of my friends had noticed him.

"Last year our team was one of the best around," Coach said. "And from what I've seen today, I think we have the potential to have an even better team then we had last year."

Ten guys—actually nine guys and one girl—from last year's team were here. I think the ten of us stood head and shoulders above the rest, other than Ashton. I didn't think we'd have much trouble making the team. Although I always worried until I was told I'd made it. I hated tryouts.

"How many of you are tired?" Coach asked.

I knew this trick. If you didn't put up your hand, that meant that you hadn't worked hard enough. Almost everybody in the gym, and every single person from last year's team, put up their hand.

"If you're new and you didn't put up your hand, you didn't work hard enough today," Coach said. "And if you're back from last year and you did put up your hand, then you didn't train hard enough over the summer."

"What?" Kia exclaimed.

"You didn't work hard enough over the summer," Coach replied. "You know how hard I work my players and you didn't get prepared." He paused. "Today was nothing compared to what it will be like if you make the team. If you thought this was hard, you better rethink if you want to be on this team. If you still want to play, I'll see you back here next Sunday at one."

We all walked over to the bleachers to get water, change and retrieve our stuff.

"What's with your dad?" I asked L.B., Coach's son.

"Nothing," he said, shaking his head. "He's actually in a good mood. You know him, he's just trying to set a tone for the season. Who's that kid talking to Kia?"

"That's Ashton. He's sort of a friend of ours."

"Sort of?"

"We just met him a couple of days ago. He can play ball."

"He's good," L.B. said. "Really good."

"L.B.!" Coach bellowed. "These balls aren't picking themselves up!"

"Later," he said to me and walked over to give his father some help.

I grabbed my stuff and walked over to join Kia. By the time I got there, Ashton had already gone.

"Did you tell him how well he did?" I asked.

"He told me how well he did," she replied.

"He certainly doesn't lack confidence," I said. "Is he coming back next week?"

"He said he was," she replied.

"Good to hear. You hungry?"

"When have you known me not to be hungry?" Kia asked. "Do you think your dad will take us for something to eat?"

"Are you kidding? You know my dad. He's the king of the drive-through. Hurry up and get changed."

We said goodbye to everybody in the gym and rushed outside. My father was sitting in our car, waiting for us. He helped out with the team last year, but like all parents he wasn't even allowed into the practices until the team had been picked.

"Well?" he asked as we jumped in.

"It went okay," I said.

"Does it look like you two might make the team?"

"It's in the bag. Guaranteed we're on the team," Kia said.

"Coach Barkley said that?" my father asked.

"Of course not. We made first cut, that's all," I answered.

"Trust me," Kia said. She turned to me. "Nick?"

"Oh, yeah. Dad, do you think we could stop on the way home and get something to eat?"

"If we get something, will you absolutely, positively guarantee me that you'll eat all your supper?" my father asked.

"Sure...I guess...what are we having?"

"I have no idea," he said, "but whatever it is, your mother is making it, and if we have fast food and then you don't eat her home cooking, it won't just be you she'll be mad at. So you have to promise you'll eat it, no matter what it is."

"Okay, I promise."

"Then we can get some food. Let's go."

We did up our seat belts and started off.

"Any new kids who look good?" my father asked.

"Yeah, that kid we met last week and invited to the tryout," Kia said. "His name is—there he is!"

Ashton was walking along the side of the road.

"I guess he must live around here," my father said.

"No, he doesn't," I said. "He goes to school at Brookmeade, so he lives pretty far from here."

"Maybe he'd like a ride," my father offered. He pulled over.

I jumped out of my door and waved my hands over my head. "Hey, Ashton!" I yelled. He waved back. "You want a ride?"

He smiled and ran to the car. "Thanks," he said. He climbed into the car and I climbed in after him.

"Ashton, you've already met my mom. This is my dad," I said.

"Pleased to meet you, sir, and thanks for the ride."

"That's no problem," my father said as he pulled the car back into traffic.

"What happened, didn't your ride show up?" Kia asked.

He shook his head. "I didn't have a ride. I was walking home."

"From here?" I asked in shock. "You were walking home from here?"

"Yeah."

"But that would take forever," Kia said.

"Less than an hour."

"It's got to take a lot longer than that," she said.

He shook his head. "That's how long it took me to walk here this morning."

"You walked here?" I asked, not believing my ears. My parents hardly let me leave the street alone.

"That explains why you were late," Kia said.

"And that's not a good thing," I added. "Coach hates late."

"I guess I'll have to leave earlier next week."

"Or we could drive you," I suggested.

"Yeah, if you want, you can come with us next week," Kia agreed.

"That's okay. It's not that far and I don't want to put anybody out."

"You wouldn't be putting us out," my father said. "I insist."

"Thank you, sir," he said.

"Of course, it won't be me next week. It'll be Nick's mother."

"Are you away again?" I asked.

"I'm afraid so. I'm heading out to the West Coast on Wednesday and I won't be back until late Sunday night."

"I wish you weren't away so much lately," I said.

"Me too. That's why I can't help out with the team this year. I'm just on the road too much. But enough of that. We have one more stop to make before we get you kids home. So what's it going to be?" my father asked.

"Wendy's," Kia said.

"Definitely Wendy's," I agreed.

"I hope you don't mind if we stop for a minute to grab a bite," my father said to Ashton. "We won't be long. We'll go to the drive-through window."

Wendy's was just up ahead. My father pulled into the parking lot and then into the drive-through lane.

"Now, I know what I want," my father said, "and I'm assuming you two want your regular."

"For sure," I said.

"Yep," Kia agreed.

"So all I need to know is what you want, Ashton."

"I'm okay."

"No, really, you must at least need a drink," my father said. "If I know Coach Barkley, he made sure you were all worked hard enough to need a drink."

He shook his head. "I didn't bring any money."

"Money?" my father questioned. "That's my job. I always treat after basketball. It's tradition. So what will you have?"

"I guess a Coke, thanks."

"Only a drink?" I asked. "You have to be hungry after working as hard as you did today. And that's not even mentioning the walk to get here."

"He's right," my father agreed. "Tell you what. I'll order another Classic Single Combo, and if you don't want the burger and fries, I'm sure Nick or Kia or I can finish it off."

"Thanks."

"So what do you want on your burger?" my father asked.

"Just lettuce and onions, please."

"That's just like Nick!" Kia exclaimed.

"Good choice," I agreed.

My father placed the order and it was waiting for us by the time we got to the window. They handed him the bags and drinks, and he handed them back for us to sort out.

"Nothing like a cold Coke and a burger after working out," my father said.

"Working out?" I asked. "What workout did you do?"

"Well...maybe we could have a little game on the driveway when we get home. That is, if you're not too tired or too scared."

"Me, scared of you? You're on," I said.

We drove along in silence, the only sound the chewing of burgers and fries and slurping of our pops.

"Ashton, you have to help me out. Where exactly do you live?"

"Two hundred Slateview."

"I know the street. Where is your house?"

"It's not a house. It's an apartment. It's one of the big towers in the complex."

"Okay, then I do know where you live," my father said.

"Yeah, I guess everybody knows the towers," Ashton said.

"You can actually see them from here," my father said.

I bent down slightly so I could peer out through the front windshield. Up ahead loomed four tall apartment towers. Ashton was right. Everybody did know those towers and rows of townhouses that surrounded them. Most people in town just called them "the complex." I was under orders never to go in there. But then again, I was pretty much not allowed to ever go anywhere farther than the end of my driveway without permission.

The real downside to having a mother who worked for the newspaper was that she seemed to know all the bad things that happened in town and where they took place. And apparently lots of those bad things happened in that complex.

"Which building is yours?" Kia asked.

"The one on the right. The tallest. I just hope the elevators are working today."

"Were they broken?" Kia asked.

"Yesterday. I didn't even check this morning. I just took the stairs down."

My father slowed the car down as we came to the entrance of the complex. I'd driven by it dozens and dozens of times, but I'd never been inside there.

"This is good," Ashton said. "There's lots of speed bumps and it can get a little confusing getting out again."

My father stopped just past the entrance. "Are you sure this is okay?"

"This is perfect," Ashton said.

I climbed out of the car to let him out. He

got out and then leaned back into the open door. "Thanks for the ride, sir. And the meal. I really appreciate it."

"It's my pleasure. And remember, if you need a ride, you just call."

"Thanks."

"You do have our number, right?"

"No, I don't."

"Nick, write it down for your friend," my father said.

"You don't have to write it down," he said. "Just say it to me. I have this thing with numbers. I can remember them."

I said our telephone number and Ashton repeated it back to me.

"We'll see you next week," I said and got back in the car.

We drove away and I looked back as Ashton walked into the complex. I couldn't help but think how different his world was from mine. How very different.

4

I bent over at the waist, my chest heaving up and down, up and down, trying to catch my breath. Coach was running us like there was no tomorrow. I guessed that was the idea. For everybody except twelve of us there wasn't going to be a tomorrow because he was picking the team after this tryout.

"Is it...is it always...like this?" Ashton panted out.

"Not always, but he does work us hard."

"Hard doesn't describe it," he said. "But he does seem to know his stuff."

"He should. He played in the NBA."

"He did?" Ashton asked. He turned around and looked at Coach.

"A couple of seasons."

"He does look like he could play some ball. Except for that leg. He's got a limp."

"That limp is what stopped him from being a star. Blew up his knee so badly that even surgery couldn't fix it."

"So what's he doing here, you know, coaching kids?" Ashton asked.

"He's coaching his kid. L.B. is his son."

"Which one is that?" Ashton asked.

I pointed him out.

"That explains why he was giving that kid such a hard time. Fathers and big brothers are always toughest on their own family."

"Coach can be pretty tough on everybody," I said.

"When he started bugging me about losing the ball that time I was gonna tell him to shut up," Ashton said.

"What?" I gasped, unable to believe what he had just said.

"I was gonna tell him to shut up," he repeated. "You know when he said something about how there are other people on the team and I should pass more, I was just going to let him have it. Do you remember him saying that?"

"Yeah, I remember." Of course I remembered, because I was one of those people on his team who he didn't seem to want to pass to.

"Look, Ashton," I said. "You're a good player and I think you can make the team, but if you ever told Coach to shut up, you'd probably be smart to just grab your bag and leave. He demands respect."

"Then he should give it," Ashton said.

"He does respect us. He tries to treat everybody well, but he wants you to become the best player you can be. Even if you're annoyed with him, you have to button it."

Ashton didn't say anything.

It was okay that he didn't answer because there were lots of things I wasn't going to tell him about last year.

When Coach first started as our coach, he was really hard on us. A lot harder than he was this year and harder in a different way. So hard, in fact, that we all quit—the whole team, including his son. We just told him we didn't want to play for him. He'd learned from that. He was still tough and demanding, and his voice was so loud that he could shatter glass, but as long as we were doing our best, working hard, he was happy. At least as happy as he could be. He still wanted to win, but he could accept losing if we worked hard.

"Do you really think I'm doing good?" Ashton asked.

I nodded. "Really good. But it wouldn't hurt if you passed more. Look for the open man." It also wouldn't hurt if he'd hustle back on defense, but I wasn't going to add that.

"Okay, everybody!" Coach barked out. "Gather around for another minute before you go home."

A much smaller group of kids gathered around him. Some kids hadn't come back after the first tryout and others had been "talked to" by Coach and told they'd been cut during this tryout. Those left were the only people still in the running for the team. I tried to do a quick head count.

"If you look around," Coach said, "you'll see that there aren't many of you left. Only fifteen people to fill twelve spots."

That answered that question.

"There's nobody here who isn't good enough to be on the team. Nobody. Unfortunately I'm only allowed to keep twelve players. That means that three of you, three very good players, aren't going to make the team."

A shudder went up my spine. I hated cuts. I hated the idea of being cut. Had I shown enough to stay? Was I one of the twelve or one of the three?

"Sometimes it has nothing to do with how well you play, but how well you play as part of a team," he continued.

That made me feel better—I was a good team player. And then I suddenly felt worse. I wanted Ashton to make it, but was he a team player? I didn't think so.

"In the next few days you'll get a call from me either to tell you that you made the team or to thank you for coming out. Either way, it's been a pleasure to have you here and, like I said, you're all good ball players. Thanks."

Coach closed his folder and walked away, leaving us standing there. The new kids all went over to get their bags, and the ten of us from last year's team just stood there.

"I think we're all okay," Tristan said. "Well, at least I know I'm okay."

"I think we're all okay," Kia added. "He knows we can play, individually and as a team."

There was a general nodding of heads and mumbling of agreement.

"Well, if he keeps all of us," Jamie said, "who do you think he's going to cut?"

We all turned and looked toward the five kids gathering their things by the bleachers.

"I think he'll keep Ashton," Kia said.

"Yeah, he can play," David said.

"He's got some moves," Jordan agreed.

"That doesn't mean anything," L.B. said, and we all turned to him. "Didn't you hear what my father said? He's looking for the best team player, not necessarily the best player. The kid can play, maybe better than most of us, but can he play as a member of a team?"

Nobody answered, although I guess that was sort of an answer. I felt sad. I didn't really know him that well, but I thought he could add something to the team. Besides, I liked him, and I knew Kia liked him too.

Silently kids started to move off to get their stuff.

"I'll meet you at the car," I said to Kia.

"At the car? Where are you going?"

"I want to talk to Coach."

"It won't do you any good," she said. "He's not going to tell you if you made the team."

"I don't want to know if I made the team."

"You going to ask about Ashton?" she asked.

I nodded. I was never surprised when Kia knew what I was thinking or going to do. Actually I was more surprised when she didn't know.

Coach Barkley was chasing down loose balls and putting them into the mesh bags.

"You got a minute, Coach?" I asked.

"I've got all the time in the world for you, Nick."

"I was just wondering if I could ask you a question."

"Shoot."

Now that I had permission, I didn't know if I had the words. "When you talked about a player being a good team player more than just a good player..."

"Yep, that's important. And you have nothing to worry about there. You are a good team player."

"Thanks, Coach."

"But you know I can't tell you if you made the team. That wouldn't be fair to everybody else."

"That's not what I wanted to ask you," I said.

"It isn't?"

I shook my head. "I just wanted to know about Ashton."

"I can't tell you if he made the team either," he said.

"I know. It's just that he really is a good guy, and maybe sometimes he doesn't play like there are other guys out there, but that's because he's never played organized ball, and if he made the team I'd help him understand."

"That's very nice of you," Coach said. "But you're assuming that you made the team."

"Me?" I gasped. "You mean I didn't make the team?"

"I didn't say that," Coach said and started to chuckle. "You really have to lighten up. Don't worry about your friend, and don't worry about you either."

"You mean I made the team?"

"I mean don't worry. Just go home, have a cool drink, finish your homework and wait for my call. Okay?"

"Okay. Sure. Thanks." I turned and started to walk away.

"Hey, Nick!"

I turned back around.

"Coming over to ask showed some guts, as well as what a good team player you are. Talk to you later on tonight. And Nick, don't worry."

"Um...sure...thanks."

If I could believe what he'd just said, I really didn't have to worry. I was on the team. So was Ashton. Probably. Maybe. I guess. I knew I'd still worry until I got the call.

5

I grabbed the rebound and fed it out to the next player waiting in line to take a lay-up. We were almost finished our warm-ups. As always I had one eye on our team and the other on the team warming up at the far end of the gym. I always wanted to know what they had and who I had to worry about.

I glanced over at the clock on the scorer's table. The time was ticking down and there was less than two minutes until the game would start. It was just an exhibition game, but it was still a game, our first game of the year, and I was feeling nervous. Heck, who was I fooling? I'd feel nervous if this was our seventy-first game. I always felt nervous before a game.

I didn't know if anybody else on the team felt that way. I could always ask though. It wasn't like they were strangers. It was a new year, but it was hardly a new team. All the players from last year's squad were on the team. There were only two new guys.

"Your turn, Nick," Ashton said.

I looked over at him.

"The ball. It's your turn to go."

I took the bounce pass and put up a right-handed lay-up. Nice and easy and into the net.

Ashton, who'd been behind me in the line, took the next pass. He dribbled in and put up a reverse lay-up. It looked really fancy, but the ball bounced off the rim instead of going in. That was Ashton. He wanted to be fancy—even if it didn't work. He trotted over and took up the spot behind me in the rebounding line.

"You okay?" Ashton asked.

"Sure. Why wouldn't I be?"

"You just look a little bit off...like you're not paying attention...or even a little bit scared," he said.

"I'm certainly not scared. Maybe a little nervous. A little. I always am before a game. You?"

"Me?" he asked, sounding genuinely surprised that I'd even ask the question. "The only way I'd be nervous is if I was playing against me."

I laughed. I knew he was joking. Well, sort of joking. Ashton had lots of confidence. He reminded me of Kia. No matter what the question, problem or game, she figured she could answer it, solve it or win it. Usually she could, and the times it didn't go her way she was genuinely surprised.

"I've been watching those guys taking their warm-ups, and there's nobody down there we have to worry much about," Ashton said.

"You're right, we don't," I agreed.

"You been watching them too?"

"I always check out the other team. It gives you an advantage when the game starts."

"That's what my biggest brother always says," Ashton said.

"Does he play ball?"

"All my brothers play ball. All of them."

51

"How many brothers do you have?" I asked.

"Four. I'm the baby, but my mother told me that if I was her first child instead of her fifth, I'd probably be her only child."

I laughed out loud.

"I told her if I was her first, there wouldn't be a need for any others because once you've found perfection, what more can you do?"

"I guess we'll find out how perfect you are tonight."

"I'll be really perfect against these guys," he said.

"Actually we were perfect against them last year. We played them four times and won all four games."

"Close games?" he asked.

"The closest had us winning by over twenty points."

The pre-game buzzer sounded and we all stopped and went over to the bench where Coach was waiting.

"If the warm-ups are any indication, I think we're going to have a very good game," Coach said. "I know we've beaten this team every time we've played them, but it's important not to get overconfident. If you look over at the scoreboard, you'll notice the score is zero-zero. Nothing that happened last year matters. Fresh game, fresh score."

He was right about us being confident. Everybody was really loose, joking around, like there was no way we could lose to this team. But nothing was definite. We could lose.

"I want you all to look back at the scoreboard. Now add a two to the score of the other team. No, I don't mean like they're up by two. I mean like there's a two in front of their zero. The score right now is twenty for them and nothing for us. I want us to play like we're down by twenty points at the tip-off. So if we don't win by at least twenty-one points, we've lost this game."

"Twenty-one points?" Ashton asked. "If we want we can beat this sorry bunch by fifty points!"

There was hooting and hollering out agreement.

"He's right," Coach said. "We might be able to take them by that much, but we're not going to. A twenty-point win sends a message that we're good. Beating them by fifty points says we're a bunch of bad sports. A twenty-one–point win will be just fine." He paused. "I want to start with Jordan at center, David power forward, Kia at small forward, Tristan at shooting point and Jamie at point guard. Now go out and give us a good start."

The five of them went out onto the court and the rest of us took to the bench. Coach walked over to talk to the refs. He always wished them good luck before a game. That was probably wise because during and after the game he usually had nothing good to say to or about them. At least he was getting better at not saying anything to them, but I could tell when he wanted to say something.

It would start with the ref making some call—usually against us—and Coach would puff out his cheeks and start pacing around, and then finally he'd turn and face away from the game, like he was pretending the ref wasn't really there. That seemed to work most of the time. Twice, when he didn't and he'd yelled out something, he'd been given technical fouls. Once he'd been tossed and my father had to take over the team for the rest of the game.

"This really sucks," Ashton said under his breath.

"What?" I asked.

"It isn't fair."

"What isn't fair?"

"I should be starting," he said.

"Don't worry about it."

"I'm not worried. It's just wrong. The best players should start and I'm one of the best players," Ashton persisted.

I wanted to change the subject before somebody else on the bench—Coach or another player—heard him talking like this.

"Is your brother here?" I asked, gesturing to the bleachers on the far side of the court. Ashton had mentioned that one of his brothers might be at the game.

"I don't see him," he said. "He said he'd be late if he could make it. Maybe it's better that he doesn't show up at all."

"Why not? Do you get nervous playing in front of him?"

"I don't get nervous about nothing. Just don't want him to come all this way to see me sitting. He can see me do that on my living room couch."

"You'll get a chance to be out there soon. On this team everybody gets playing time. Some coaches just use five or six players. He plays everybody."

"Then he should have played me to start."

"Sit tight, stop complaining and be ready when Coach calls your number," I said.

"Nick, Ashton, L.B., get ready to go in," Coach said.

I pulled off my sweat top, got up off the bench and headed for the scorer's table.

"Told you we'd get in," I said to Ashton as I bent down beside him.

"About time. The first quarter is almost over."

"The game is practically over," L.B. said.

Of course he didn't mean the time, but the result was pretty well decided. We were already up seventeen to seven. We were well on the way to getting back that imaginary twenty points that the other team had to start the game.

The ball went out of bounds and the ref signaled for the change to take place. We gave high fives to D.J., Mark and Tristan as they came off and we went on.

I walked over to the ref. He handed me the ball and blew his whistle to start play. I passed the ball in to Ashton. He started dribbling the ball up court. He broke to one side and then to the other. Jordan cut for the net, his hands up. He was completely in the clear. Ashton didn't see him. He dribbled over to the other side of the court. I flashed through and Ashton ignored me as well.

Finally he broke around a screen that L.B. had set and cut in for the net. A player tried to block him and he put up an underhanded circus shot that hit the backboard and dropped in for a bucket! You could almost hear the other side gasp as the ball dropped. It was an incredible shot.

The other team started back up the court. Ashton was all over their ball carrier. He reached out and hit the ball—and the player's arm! The ref blew his whistle.

"Foul, number one, two, orange!"

"Foul!" Ashton yelled. "What are you talking about? That was nothing but ball!"

"Technical foul!" the ref yelled. "One shot and they get the ball back!"

Ashton looked like he was going to say something more to the ref. I grabbed him by the arm and pulled him down the court.

"Shut up," I hissed.

"Who are you telling to shut up?" Ashton asked.

"You...now just shut up and walk back."

Ashton didn't say anything, but he didn't fight me. I led him down the court.

We waited at center while their player took his foul shot.

He put up the shot and it was an air ball. Ashton laughed out loud and slapped me on the back.

"Sub!" Coach called out. Sean was standing beside the scorer's table so I knew who was coming in. I also knew who was going out.

"Ashton!" Coach called.

"Me?" Ashton asked.

"Yeah, you...you're out."

Ashton shot Coach a dirty look and for a second I thought he was going to actually refuse to leave the court. He walked over—no, he swaggered over—and sat down at the very end of the bench, as far away from Coach as he could get. I thought that was probably a good idea. Hopefully Ashton would have a chance to think about why he'd been taken off. I'd talk to him after the game, just to make sure he understood.

"That was a pretty convincing win," my father said as we drove home.

"Twenty-five points isn't bad," I agreed.

"It could have been fifty," Ashton said. "More if he'd have let me play more."

Ashton hadn't got back on again until the end of the second quarter. And then he played like there was nobody else on the court. At least nobody else on his side. I could count the passes he made on the fingers of one hand. Actually, I knew people were counting and grumbling.

"You're lucky he let you play as much as he did," I said.

"What do you mean by that?" Ashton demanded.

"You can't be doing things like that."

"Things like what?" Ashton asked.

"Come on, you know."

"Know what?"

"The technical foul was bad enough, but he took you off because you laughed at that guy's air ball."

"But it was funny. Besides, it's basketball, not ballet. Trash talking goes with the game."

"You really don't know Coach very well, do you?"

"And he doesn't know me," Ashton replied.

My father pulled the car off to the side of the road. We were in front of Ashton's complex. He grabbed his bag.

My father turned around in his seat. "You didn't play much, but you played well."

"Thanks. And thanks for the ride, sir."

"Never a problem. Do you need a ride for Tuesday?"

"Tuesday?" Ashton asked.

"Practice," I said. "Every Tuesday. Do you need a ride?"

"I think so. Probably."

"I'll give you a call to check," I said.

"It'll be Nick's mother doing the driving," my father said.

"Are you gone again?" I asked. I was tired of him being gone so much.

"Afraid so."

Ashton started to climb out of the car.

"Oh, by the way," my father said. "We have to have all the registration papers back and the rep money collected. Can you bring a check on Tuesday and give it to Nick's mom. She's the manager of the team this year."

"Sure...okay," Ashton answered. He sounded uneasy, unsure.

Ashton closed the door.

As we drove away I looked out the back window and watched him walk into the complex.

6

"Let's wrap it up!" Coach yelled. "That was a good practice. Everybody worked really hard!"

I walked over to the bleachers to get my stuff.

"Those of us who were here worked hard," Kia said to me. "What happened to Ashton? Where is he?"

I shook my head. "I called him—twice—and left messages. I told him we'd pick him up if he needed a ride, but he didn't even call back."

"Maybe he forgot," Kia said. "Or maybe there was an emergency or something."

"I don't know. I don't know anything."

"Nick! Kia!" Coach called. We turned to face him and he motioned for us to come over.

"Did we do anything wrong?" I asked Kia under my breath.

"I know I didn't do anything wrong...but you?"

"Shut up."

We trotted over to Coach.

"I was wondering if either of you know what happened to Ashton."

"No idea," Kia said.

"I called him. Maybe he had problems with a ride or something," I suggested.

"Maybe. If either of you talks to him—"

"I'll be talking to him for sure," I said.

"Get him to call me."

"Sure, no problem."

"Is your father picking you up, Nick?"

"My mother."

"Is your father out of town again?" Coach asked.

"Yeah."

"Too bad. I was still hoping he might be able to help me out again this year."

"I know he really wants to help...it's just that he's gone so much."

Coach nodded his head. "Yep. Too bad. See you two on Saturday. Hopefully I'll see the whole team."

"Yeah, bye, Coach."

We hurried off.

"I thought he'd be really angry at Ashton," Kia said.

"I'm not sure he isn't. He's still pretty tough on everybody, but he doesn't get mad at us the way he did at the beginning of last season."

"That's good, but the important thing is that, even if he is mad at Ashton, he isn't mad at us."

"So how was practice?" my mother asked as we climbed into the car.

"It was good," I said. "Tiring but good."

"Yeah, I'm beat," Kia agreed.

"Does Ashton need a ride home?" my mother asked.

"He wasn't even there tonight," I answered.

"He wasn't?" she asked.

"Nope. No show and no call."

"Gee, I hope he isn't sick," my mother said.

"And I hope he *is* sick," I said.

"You do?" she asked. "Why would you hope he was sick?"

"Sick is better than dead."

"Good heavens, why would you even think that he might be dead?" my mother questioned.

"Because he didn't call Coach to say he wouldn't be there," I explained. "Coach might kill him."

"Don't be so dramatic," she said.

"Who's being dramatic?" I asked.

"You are. You don't actually think that Coach Barkley is going to kill him, do you?"

"Not kill him dead, but cut him from the team dead."

"That's almost as bad," Kia said.

"He's not going to cut him for one missed practice. You both missed a couple of practices last season," she said.

"We missed practice for a good reason and we called and explained why. You called and explained why I couldn't come."

"Maybe Ashton asked somebody to call and they forgot," my mother said. "I don't even know who's in his family."

"I don't know either, exactly," I said. "I just know he has four older brothers."

"Five boys?" my mother said. "That must be quite the active house."

"Sounds like a nightmare to me," Kia said and she and my mother started to laugh.

They were having one of their little "times" that they said I couldn't really understand because I was a boy. I was pretty sure I was happy I didn't understand.

"Are you coming over to the house for a snack?" my mother asked Kia.

"I'd like to, but I have to get home. I still have to practice piano."

"That reminds me," my mother said. "Nick, did you do your piano today?"

"Not yet," I answered. I shot Kia a dirty look and she mouthed "sorry."

"Then I guess we know what you'll be doing when we get home," my mother said.

We pulled up to Kia's house. Kia climbed out, thanked my mother and ran up the driveway. We sat there, waiting until she reached the house. My mother would never drive away until she knew Kia was safe. Kia opened the door and waved goodbye. We drove away.

"Is it alright if I make a phone call before I start my piano?" I asked.

"Who are you going to call?"

"Ashton."

"As long as the call isn't too long. I don't want this to be some kind of excuse so that you don't have to practice piano tonight."

"It won't take long," I reassured her. "I just want to see if he's—there he is!"

"There is who?" my mother exclaimed.

"Ashton! He's there in the park...sitting on one of the swings!"

I peered out through the back window as we continued to drive.

"Are you sure that's him?" she asked.

"Of course I'm sure!"

"What is he doing here?"

"I don't know. I just know that he's there. Can I go back and talk to him?"

My mother pulled into our driveway.

"Can I go back?" I asked again.

"For a few minutes. And let him know, if he needs a ride home, that I can give him one...His place is a long way from here and it's getting late...It'll be dark soon."

"Thanks, Mom, thanks a lot."

I jumped out of the car and ran back down the street. The swings were empty. Had he gone or had I not really seen him? Then I saw him sitting on the edge of a picnic bench.

"Ashton!" I yelled and he waved back. I ran up to him. "Where were you?"

"Lots of places. Right now I'm here."

"I mean why weren't you at practice?" I asked.

"Why should I show up for practice when I don't get to play?" he demanded.

"You got to play."

"I hardly got to play. If I'm going to sit instead of play, I might as well just sit at home instead of practicing."

"I told you, you'll get playing time," I said. "You got playing time during the game. Look, you have to come to practice if you want to be on the team."

"Who says I want to be on the team?" he replied.

"What did you say?" I asked, not believing the words he'd just spoken.

"Who says I even want to be on the team?" he repeated.

"What are you talking about? You want to be on the team."

"Maybe I wanted to be on the team, but that doesn't mean I want to be on it now."

"Of course you want to be on the team. Don't be stupid."

"Who are you calling stupid?" Ashton demanded as he jumped off the bench. He clenched his fists and his face took on a serious, almost threatening look.

"Well, who are you calling stupid?" he repeated.

I took a deep breath. "There's nobody else here but you, so I must be talking to you."

Ashton sat back down on the bench and looked away from me. "I don't even want to talk about this," he said.

"You don't?" I asked.

"No, I don't."

70

"You're wrong."

"First I'm stupid and now I'm wrong."

"You are if you think you don't want to talk about it because I know you do."

"I do? What are you, a psychic or something? You can read my mind?" he questioned.

"Not your mind, but isn't it obvious why you're here?"

"I'm stupid, so how can anything be obvious to me?" Ashton asked. "I'm just hanging around. I was swinging," he said. "That's why I'm here."

"And there are no swings between here and your complex?"

"No, there's swings right in the complex, right beside my apartment."

"Then why are you here, way away from your place?"

He didn't answer right away. "Maybe I was looking for a quiet place."

"Or maybe you were hoping to run into me so I could convince you to come back to the team."

He didn't answer again, but he sat back down on one of the swings.

71

"It doesn't really matter. I'm never going to get much playing time. I can tell."

"How can you tell that?" I asked.

"I just know. That coach doesn't like me."

"What do you mean he doesn't like you?"

"He's always telling me I'm doing things wrong, telling me I need to pass more and how I don't shoot the ball very well. He's always giving me a hard time. He just plain doesn't like me."

"He's hard on everybody. That's the way he coaches. It isn't personal."

"I think it is. He's harder on me then he is on anybody else...well, anybody except his kid," Ashton said.

"And I guess he's hard on his kid because he doesn't like him either," I argued.

"No. It's just...just..."

"Look, Ashton, I know he likes you."

"Yeah, right."

"He does."

"What makes you think that?" Ashton asked. "Another psychic guess?"

"I know he likes you because he told me."

"He did?"

I nodded. Actually he'd never said that, but I knew that Coach liked everybody on his team, so I wasn't really telling a lie.

"So he does like me?" Ashton sounded like he didn't really believe me, but he wanted to.

"He does. Besides, sometimes a coach is hardest on the people he thinks have the most potential," I said. "Have you ever thought of that?"

"Not really."

"Then you should think about it." It was also possible that he was hardest on Ashton because he deserved it the most. The kid could learn to pass a little more. "Look, it's getting late. My mother said she'd give you a ride home if you needed one."

"That's okay, I don't want to bother anybody."

"It's not a bother. Do you need a ride to practice on Saturday?"

He didn't answer. He just sat there, staring ahead.

"You are coming to practice on Saturday, right?"

"I...I don't know."

"What do you mean you don't know? Haven't you been listening to anything I've said?"

"I've been listening!" he snapped.

"Then why wouldn't you go to practice?"

"Because there's no point."

"What do you mean there's no point? That doesn't make sense. To be part of the team you have to go to practices."

"To be part of the team you have to pay the registration fees," Ashton said.

"Of course you have to pay the..." I stopped myself. I hadn't even thought about that. I never had to think about things like that.

"It's a lot of money," Ashton said. "Like three hundred and fifty dollars."

"It doesn't have to be that much," I said.

"It doesn't?"

"No, it depends on the fund-raising money."

"Fund-raising? What fund-raising?"

"We sell boxes of chocolate-covered almonds to support the team. Every box somebody sells, they get to pay one dollar less on their registration fees."

"Like a dollar or two is going to help," Ashton snorted.

"Not a dollar or two. If you sell a lot of almonds, you raise a lot of money."

"I'd have to sell three hundred and fifty boxes. There's no way I could ever sell that many."

"Maybe not by yourself. But how about if you had some help?"

"You offering to help me?" Ashton asked.

"Why not? My registration is already paid."

"And you'd help me?"

"Me and Kia."

He shrugged. "I don't know."

"What don't you know? We're teammates, and teammates help each other. How about you come over to my place right after school tomorrow. We have the boxes of almonds for the whole team in our basement. That's part of my mother's job as manager of the team. We'll have a snack and then hit the streets."

"I don't think we can do it, even with three of us. We'd just be wasting our time."

"Maybe," I admitted. "But what have you got to lose?"

Ashton shook his head. "Nothing. I got nothing to lose. I'll see you tomorrow." He jumped off the swing and started to walk away.

"You sure you don't want a ride?" I called after him.

"Nope. It's not far. See you tomorrow."

I watched Ashton walk away. Maybe I'd given him some hope. Now I just wished I believed that we could actually sell three hundred and fifty boxes of almonds.

7

Kia knocked on the door and we waited for an answer. It didn't take long. The door swung open and a woman—about my mother's age—answered.

"Hello, we're members of the Mississauga Magic basketball team. We're selling chocolate-covered almonds," Kia said, holding up one of the boxes.

All three of us stood there, smiling, wearing our orange basketball jerseys. Actually Ashton was wearing one of my old jerseys because we hadn't got our new uniforms yet.

"How much are they?" the woman asked.

"Three dollars a box," I replied.

"That's a lot of money for a box of almonds."

"That's because there are a lot of almonds in each box," Kia replied, holding the box up even higher. "And it helps local kids."

"Are you three all on the same team?" the woman asked.

"All three of us. I'm the only girl on the team," Kia said.

"But others could play," I added. "Our team believes in equality for girls and boys."

"That's excellent!" the woman said. "How about if I take two...no, make it three...one from each of you."

"Thank you, ma'am," Ashton said. "Thanks a lot."

The woman reached into her pocket and pulled out a ten-dollar bill. She handed the bill to Kia, who passed over three boxes. I dug into my box and found a dollar to give her as change.

"No, that's alright. You keep the change," she said.

"Thank you so much!" I beamed.

"It's my pleasure. Have a nice day," she said as she closed the door.

"That was really good," Kia said. "That was like selling four boxes because we made four dollars."

"We are doing amazingly well," I said.

"We are," Ashton agreed. "How many have we sold?"

"If you count these three, I mean four, that makes almost one hundred boxes sold," I said.

"That is pretty good," Kia agreed. "Has anybody ever sold that many before?"

"Not from our team, at least as far as I know. But we still have a lot farther to go."

"You gotta stop looking at this from the negative," Kia said. "Don't think about how much farther we have to go, but how fast we've already gotten this far. We're almost one third of the way there," Kia said.

"You're right, and that is impressive," I agreed.

"But do you know what would make it go even faster?" Kia asked.

"What?" Ashton asked.

"If we split up. If we all hit different houses we could sell more boxes."

"I think we're doing pretty good this way," I said.

"You're only saying that because you don't want to do the knocking and the talking by yourself," she said.

"I don't mind talking," I argued, although she was right, I really didn't want to do it by myself.

"I think we should stick together too," Ashton agreed.

"Come on, it isn't like you're afraid to talk," Kia said.

"No. I just don't think it would work with me walking up to these houses by myself," he said.

"Why wouldn't it?" she asked.

"I don't know if you two have noticed, but I'm black."

"Really?" Kia said. "I just thought you had a really, really good tan."

"Funny."

"So you're black, what's your point?" Kia asked.

"All of these houses, all of these people in this neighborhood are white," Ashton said.

"Not all of them. There are black people who live in this neighborhood."

"I haven't seen any."

"But there are," I repeated. "It only seems like we've been to every house in the neighborhood."

"David and Jordan and Jamie and Tristan all live around here," Kia said.

"They do?"

"And the last time I checked, unless they all have really, really good tans too, they're black as well," Kia said.

"Okay, then maybe there are a few black families here, but that doesn't mean the rest of the people aren't going to be scared of me if I'm pounding on their door."

"Who's pounding? Most of these houses have doorbells," she said.

"You know what I mean," Ashton said.

"Besides, do you really think anybody is going to be scared of you?"

Ashton didn't answer, but he gave Kia his best attempt at a mean look. She chuckled and his look dissolved into a smirk.

"If you don't want to sell almonds around

here, we could always go to your neighbor-hood," Kia suggested.

Ashton burst out laughing. "Now that's a bright idea."

"What's wrong with it?" Kia questioned.

"For starters, you two would be just as out of place in my complex as I am here."

"What do you mean?" Kia asked.

"You know all those black people who don't live in this neighborhood? Well, they all live in mine."

"Everybody in your neighborhood is black?" I asked.

"Not everybody. There are some East Indians, Chinese and even a few whites—but not a lot."

"There are all of those in this neighbor-hood. All of everybody," I said.

"Maybe so, but it still wouldn't be smart. How much money you have in that little carton you're carrying?" Ashton asked me.

"I guess close to three hundred dollars," I said under my breath, as if I was afraid that somebody would hear, even though there was nobody in sight.

"That's a lot of money. Too much money for three kids to walk around with in my neighborhood," Ashton said.

"I'm beginning to think that's too much money for three kids to walk around with in any neighborhood. How about if we head back to my place and drop off the money so we don't have to carry it around?"

"That sounds like a good idea," Kia said. "Do you think we could get a snack while we're there?"

"Like muffins, maybe?" Ashton added.

"Muffins I can't guarantee. Food I can. Let's head home."

As we started off, I became more aware of the money I was carrying. I hadn't really even thought about it until Ashton brought it up. It was a lot of cash and I was becoming more nervous. I started looking up and down the street, scanning the area for robbers. What exactly would robbers look like?

"So let me get this straight," Kia said. "If we were in your neighborhood, we'd get robbed?"

"We might."

"Has that ever happened to you before?" I asked.

"Me? Never."

"Have you ever seen anybody being robbed?" I asked.

"Never."

"Do you even know anybody who has ever been robbed?" Kia persisted.

"No, but it happens. I know somebody who had their apartment broken into."

"I know lots of people in this neighborhood who have had their houses robbed," I said.

"That happens everywhere," Kia said. "It sounds like you think that crime only happens around your house."

"Well, if nothing else, we should stay around here because people have more money so they should have more cash to spend on chocolate-covered almonds," Ashton said.

"In that case maybe we should head to a neighborhood with bigger houses and fancier cars so we can sell more boxes," Kia said.

"We're doing just fine here. We still have some more time tonight, and then tomorrow and even Friday night if we need to. We're going to make it," I said.

"You really think so?" Ashton asked.

"Hey, would I lie?" I asked, still wondering if I was.

"Hey, Mom, we're back!" I yelled as we burst through the door.

"I'm in the kitchen!" she hollered back.

We kicked off our shoes.

"Do you smell it?" Kia asked.

"Smell what?" I asked.

"Smell nothing. I don't smell anything baking. I guess there are no muffins."

"Too bad," Ashton said.

"But there'll be something. It would be almost impossible to leave the house without my mother feeding you something," I said.

"My mom is the same way. She thinks I'm too skinny, so I can only imagine what she'd think of Kia."

"What do you mean by that?" Kia demanded.

"My mother would try and fatten you up. Both of you," he said, pointing at me.

"Sorry, my mom already has that job on a full-time basis."

"So how did things go?" my mother asked as we entered the kitchen.

"Good. So good we were hoping you'd hold the money."

I handed her the carton and she opened up the flaps.

"My goodness, how much money is in here?" she asked, looking shocked as she reached in and pulled out a wad of bills.

"Close to three hundred dollars," I said.

"That's amazing!" she exclaimed.

"It's good, but not good enough...not yet," I replied.

"Actually, it's better than you think it is."

"What does that mean?" Kia asked.

"It means two things. I was just on the phone with your coach."

"You were?" I asked.

"He called and wanted to know if it was definite that your father couldn't be an assistant coach this year."

"And you told him?" I asked.

"You know what I told him," she said.

I did. I'd just hoped that somehow it could have worked out. My father knew something about basketball—not like Coach did—but he knew ball, and we really, really did need an assistant. What would happen if Coach was tossed out of another game and there was nobody else left to work the bench?

"And while I was talking to him he told me two things that you three might be interested in. First, the registration fees are not due for another week, so that gives you more time to sell almonds."

"That is good news," Kia said.

"And the second thing?" I asked.

"And the second thing is that you've sold another fifty boxes of almonds," my mother said.

"We have?" I gasped.

"How? To who?" Kia questioned.

"To your coach. He bought fifty boxes."

"But why would he buy them from us?" Ashton asked. "Wouldn't he just buy them from his own son?"

"Because he's the coach, his son doesn't have to pay registration fees or sell anything.

But he told me he just loves those chocolate-covered almonds, so he bought a bunch. He said he'd like you to bring the boxes on Saturday and he'll pass on the money."

"That's great!" Kia remarked.

"That means we're almost halfway there," I said.

"Not quite," Ashton said, "but we're getting there. I bet we can sell another thirty boxes tonight if we really tried."

"Tonight? Aren't you three finished for the evening?" my mother asked.

"We were hoping we could get a snack and then head back out again," I explained.

"It's going to be dark soon," she said, "and I don't want you three out after dark. It isn't safe."

I looked at the clock up on the wall. "We have another hour before then. How about if we go right back out now for a while, and you could bake some muffins while we're gone so they'll be waiting when we return?"

"I think that can be arranged and—" She stopped talking as the phone rang. "I'll get that. It might be your father."

"You know," Kia said, "we don't even have to go back out again tonight. What with the extra time and the boxes that Coach bought, we're way ahead. What do you think?"

I looked at Ashton. Part of me—especially my very tired feet—wanted to stay here. "Well?" I asked.

"You can stay if you want," he said, "but I'm going to go back out and try to sell some more."

"Go out by yourself?" Kia asked. "I thought you were afraid you'd scare people?"

"Maybe I can scare them into buying more boxes," Ashton said and smiled.

"It doesn't matter if you scare them or not because you're not going to be by yourself." I got up from the kitchen table. "Let's go."

8

I doubled over and panted, trying to catch my breath. I pulled the bottom of my shirt up and wiped the sweat off my face. You'd have figured that after all these years of playing basketball—hundreds of games and millions of practices—it would be easier. Wrong. They were tough. Especially at the start of the season.

I tipped back my water bottle and took a long drink. The water wasn't even that cold anymore, but it still tasted good in my mouth and on the way down my throat.

"Tired?" I asked Ashton.

"Dog-tired. Wish you hadn't convinced me to come back."

"Really?"

He shook his head. "Glad to be here."

"Everybody grab a ball and get on the baseline," Coach Barkley ordered.

I quickly put down my water bottle and scrambled to get a ball. Everybody else was chasing them down too. Nobody wanted to be the last person because sometimes Coach made that person do sit-ups or push-ups. I didn't like doing push-ups at any time, but it was so much worse when everybody else was standing there, watching, counting them off as you did them.

"We're going to have a little race," Coach Barkley said. "Who do you think is the fastest person in this gym?"

Everybody yelled out names—mostly their own. I stayed quiet. Not only because I didn't know who was the fastest, but also because there was something about the look in Coach's eyes that made me wonder what he was up to. He was always full of surprises and tricks, and you had to really think about his questions before you blurted out an answer.

"You are all wrong," Coach said. "Without a doubt the fastest person here is me."

"You?" a bunch of us said in unison.

"Yeah, me. Are any of you doubting my word?"

Nobody dared to say anything, but there was doubt etched on everybody's face.

"Tristan," Coach said, "you look like you don't believe me."

"Oh, no, Coach, I would never doubt you. I'm sure you're faster than all of us...if you were driving in your car."

There was a burst of laughter and Coach shot us a hard glare that stopped the laughter just as suddenly as it had started.

"Sorry, Coach," Tristan apologized. "I know you probably were fast...you know...in your day."

"I was really fast before I blew out my knee," he agreed. "But I'm still way faster than anybody else here. Way faster. It's not even a contest."

There was a silent response as everybody was smart enough to keep their mouths shut and their expressions blank. I had no doubt that Coach was fast when he was playing, before the injury, but I'd seen him run, and that leg really held him back now. Besides, he was really, really old. He had to be in his forties at least. And even if he was faster than some of us, there was no way he was faster than everybody. Jordan practically galloped down the court. He was definitely faster than Coach was.

"Tell you what," Coach said, "let's settle this by having a little race. Me against all of you. Here's the deal. We all start on the baseline. The first one to touch his basketball against the far wall is the winner. Agreed?"

There was a mumbling of agreement.

"And to make things interesting, I think we should have a little bet on the outcome," Coach said.

"What sort of little bet?" I asked suspiciously.

Coach smiled, and that smile unnerved me. "If I win, you all spend the rest of the practice doing wind sprints and nobody complains."

"And if we win?" L.B. asked.

"If even one of you beats me, then you can just shoot around or scrimmage for the rest of the practice."

People started cheering and applauding.

"So are we going to race?" he asked.

"Hold on," I said. I still didn't completely trust what he was saying. Not that Coach would ever lie to us, but he often had a twist, a lesson he was trying to teach, and things just didn't work out the way we thought they would.

"You have a question, Nick?"

I guess he'd been reading the expression on my face. Everybody looked at me now.

"I just want to make sure I understand what's going on," I said.

"It seems pretty straight forward to me," Coach said. "Just what is it that you don't understand? First one to touch their ball against the far wall wins the race. Simple."

"And if just one of us beats you, we win," I said.

He nodded.

"And for you to win you have to beat all of us."

Again he nodded. "Sounds like you don't exactly believe what I'm saying," he said. "Don't you think I'd keep my word?"

"No, of course not," I said. "I just wanted to make sure I understood all of those words you were saying."

"Any more questions?" Coach asked.

"One. I was just wondering what would happen if we decided we didn't want to race you," I said.

"If you don't want to race then there's no problem," he said. "We'll just spend the rest of the practice doing wind sprints." He smiled, or sort of smiled. It was more like a smirk. "So you have nothing to lose by trying. If you win, you don't have to do them. Does that make sense?"

Now I knew for certain that there was a trick. I just didn't know what it was.

"Is there something still wrong, Nick?" Coach asked, trying to sound innocent.

"Yeah, there probably is...I just don't know what it is, that's all."

Coach smiled and nodded his head slowly. That meant I was probably right, but it didn't help me figure out how I was right.

"Okay, everybody, space out across the gym. We don't want you to trip over each other," Coach said.

We spread out along the baseline until we filled the whole width of the gym. Coach was right at the end, and I moved over so I was beside him—the better to keep an eye on him.

"Do we have to dribble the balls?" I asked, still trying to figure it out. Maybe he was going to tuck his under his arm and run like a football player.

"Dribble if you want, don't dribble if you want. It's up to you," Coach said.

I could dribble pretty fast, but I could run faster. I'd just carry it. Maybe that was his plan and now I'd seen through it and...no, if I'd seen through it he would have stopped us. There had to be something else.

"Everybody get ready. On the count of three. One...two...three!"

We all jumped off the line and started running and—a basketball hit the far wall with a thunderous smash and bounced back toward us! Who had thrown that ball and...it all suddenly made sense. Coach had thrown the ball, and his ball had touched the far wall before any of us could touch our ball against it.

"And we have a winner!" Coach yelled triumphantly.

Everybody stopped running. We were caught partway down the gym and coasted to a stop, having already lost.

"Put the balls in the bag and come on back here to get ready for the wind sprints!" Coach called out.

We all groaned, quietly under our breath, and did what he told us. He'd won. Maybe not fair and square, but he'd won.

"Before we start, would somebody like to explain to me what I just proved with my little race?"

"That you're smarter than us?" Tristan said.

"Hopefully we all knew that long before now."

"That you can trick us?" Kia suggested.

"That's been proved before this too. Any more suggestions?"

Nobody said anything.

"Tell you what. If any one of you can tell me what I was trying to show you, then you don't have to do the wind sprints," Coach said.

Everybody's ears perked up.

"I'd even let you scrimmage for the rest of the practice."

"Is this another trick?" Tristan asked.

"No trick. Does anybody know what point I was trying to prove?"

Everybody mumbled and looked at each other, hoping somebody would have an answer that would spare us from the dreaded wind sprints.

"Nick?" Coach asked.

I looked at him questioningly.

"You thought that something wasn't right to begin with. Have you figured it out yet?"

"Yeah, Nick, do you know?" Kia asked.

"Come on, Nick, think," Tristan said.

"Yeah, think," Kia agreed.

"You can do it," Jamie said. "Think."

Suddenly it seemed like it was my problem, and the whole team was counting on me to solve it. This was probably worse than doing the wind sprints. Now, if I couldn't come up with an answer, it would be like it was my fault.

"Well?" Coach asked.

"Um...you were...um...trying to teach us a lesson," I stammered.

"Of course I was trying to teach you a lesson. And just what lesson was that?"

"The lesson is...is...that—" Suddenly it hit me. "The lesson is that a ball can be thrown faster than anybody can carry it, so a pass is faster than dribbling."

Coach didn't answer. He just stared at me. "Yes," he said quietly.

The whole team cheered and mobbed me as if I'd just scored the winning basket in the championship game.

"Now that you've given half the answer, could you continue by giving me the rest of the answer to my question?" Coach asked.

Everybody stopped cheering.

"The rest of the answer?" I asked. I didn't have any more answer to give.

"Yes. You told me what I did, but you didn't explain to me why I did it."

"To make us look stupid," Tristan said.

"Some of you can do that without my help," Coach said. "Well, Nick?"

I didn't answer. What was the rest of the reason?

"Anybody else?" Coach asked. "To avoid wind sprints you need the whole answer."

I took a deep breath. I hoped the extra oxygen would get my brain working.

"You did it," Kia said, "because nobody is passing the ball enough."

"Thank you, Kia!" Coach said. "That is the last half of the answer. You and Nick seem to be able to complete each other's thoughts. Now I have one more question."

Oh, great. Was he going to keep asking us questions until we couldn't answer one and then we'd start the wind sprints? On the plus side, with each passing question we got closer to the end of the practice, which meant if we did finally have to do the sprints, we wouldn't have to do as many.

"Give me some other names for basketball," Coach said.

"Other names?" L.B. asked.

"Yeah, what other names does basketball go by?"

"Hoops," Tristan said. "Lots of people call it hoops."

"Yep, that's what I call it," Coach agreed.

"Round ball," Jamie said, "although I thought all balls were round."

"B-ball," Jordan added.

"Definitely," Coach agreed. "Any others?"

People shook their heads. I couldn't think of any other names.

"How about me-ball?" Coach asked.

"Me-ball?" a bunch of us questioned.

"Never," Tristan said.

"That doesn't even make sense," Kia said.

"You're right, it doesn't make sense," Coach agreed. "But that's the way you people have been playing the game so far. I see a whole lot of 'me' and not enough 'team.' If we don't start working the ball around, passing, acting like a team, we're not going anywhere. Now I'm going to divide you into two teams for a scrimmage. What I want to see is b-ball, not me-ball."

"Look for the open man!" Coach yelled.

Ashton reversed his dribble away from the double coverage but didn't look for anybody, open or covered. I broke for the net, hands in the air, practically "yelling" for the pass. He put up a shot. It hit off the front of the rim and bounced away. Jamie got the rebound. He was playing point guard for the other side. They all were wearing bright yellow pinnies to mark their team. He came up court and drove for the net. The opening closed and he backed out.

"Pass the ball!" Coach bellowed. "Find the open man."

Jamie tried to make a pass, but by the time the ball arrived, Ashton was already there for the steal. Mark raced down the court. He was way ahead of everybody. All Ashton had to do was lob the ball to him and it was a guaranteed basket and—Ashton slowed down the play and kept dribbling. He hadn't seen Mark.

"Substitution," Coach called and a shudder went up my spine. I knew exactly what was going to happen. He was going to take Ashton off and then Ashton was going to get angry and—

"Nick, come on off!" Coach yelled.

I trotted over to the bench. That certainly wasn't what I'd expected. This was probably the first time in my whole life I was happy to be taken off. I sat down and then realized that I'd come off but nobody else had gone on. My team was now playing with only four players!

I jumped up. "Coach, you didn't put anybody else on for me," I said.

"I know, Nick," he said. "Kia!" Coach yelled out. He motioned for her to come over. "Take a seat."

"But, but—"

"Sit down," he ordered.

She stepped off the court and stood beside me. We now had only three players out there. What was he doing? Ashton kept dribbling the ball. I didn't even know if he'd noticed we weren't there.

"Jordan, Mark!" Coach called out. He motioned for them to come over to the bench. They looked confused, but both came trotting over. "Sit," he said, pointing to the bench.

Ashton was now out on the court by himself facing the five opposing players.

"Where is everybody?" Ashton yelled. He'd finally noticed he was by himself.

"Keep playing!" Coach hollered back.

Ashton shrugged but kept on dribbling.

"Press the ball carrier!" Coach yelled. Three men rushed forward and surrounded Ashton. He tried to dribble through and almost made it when the ball was knocked free. He stood there while two players raced up the court and put up a lay-up.

"Keep playing!" Coach said.

"But I'm by myself!" Ashton yelled. "How can I throw it in if it's just me?"

"Figure it out."

Ashton walked to the baseline and took the ball. L.B. was standing right in front of him, guarding him. Ashton bounced the ball off his leg and then jumped in and grabbed it.

"Press! Press! Full court press!" Coach yelled.

Suddenly Ashton was surrounded by four players. He tried to dribble by them, but there were just too many and he had no place to go. They froze him in place and he lost his dribble.

"Time violation!" Coach yelled. "You took too long to bring the ball over half. That's a turnover!"

Ashton slammed the ball on the floor and it bounced high into the air.

"And that would be a technical," Coach said. "Everybody, bring it in and let's talk."

We all surrounded Coach as he stood there with one foot on the bench.

"Some of you are figuring it out," he began. "And some of you are not. This is a team game. You win or lose by using the players on the court. Why did I pull the other players off the court and leave Ashton on by himself?"

I knew the answer. I figured everybody

knew the answer, but nobody was going to say anything.

"Because you wanted me to look stupid!" Ashton snapped.

"No. Although I hope you did feel stupid out there," he replied. "Somebody tell me why I did that."

"Because Ashton wasn't using his team-mates," Tristan finally said.

"That's right. If you're not going to pass to anybody, there's no point in them even being out there. That's it for today. Practice is over. See you all on Tuesday."

9

It was one very quiet car ride home. My mother tried to get a conversation started a couple of times, but Kia and I just sat there. Ashton hadn't even said hello when he jumped into the backseat, and he hadn't said a word since then. Actually he hadn't said a word since practice ended. He just looked angry as he stared at the back of the seat in front of him.

It was hard to be centered out like that, but I knew that Coach wasn't doing it to be mean. He had talked to everybody and then he'd talked to Ashton by himself about needing to share the ball, but talking hadn't changed the way Ashton was playing. He had to do something.

Besides, it wasn't like he hadn't centered me out before. He'd done that to everybody. Maybe to his son more than anybody else on the team. But I knew that Ashton didn't want to hear that right now. He probably couldn't hear it right now, even if I told him. Sometimes the smartest thing you can do is to just shut up. I was doing that now.

"You three are awfully quiet," my mother said, trying once again to break the silence.

"We're tired," I said. I didn't want the silence broken.

"It must have been an incredibly hard practice to make you so tired that your tongues can't flap. Are Kia and Ashton coming over for a snack or am I dropping them off at home?"

"I'd like a snack," Kia said.

"Ashton, are you coming? There's a possibility I just might make some muffins."

"I've got to get home," he said. He didn't even look up.

"Maybe tomorrow. Are you three going to be selling almonds tomorrow?" she asked.

"We were thinking about— "

"Not tomorrow," Ashton said, cutting Kia off.

"We aren't?" she asked. "I thought we had agreed we were going to—"

"Something came up," he said, cutting her off again.

"What came up that's so impor—"

"I'm sure it is important," I said, cutting Kia off for the third time. Just let the guy sit. Getting him talking now might lead him to say something he'd regret—something he'd have trouble backing down from.

"Is anybody going to let me finish a sentence?" she demanded.

"You just did," I said. "If Ashton doesn't want to sell almonds tomorrow, we'll do it later. We're down to the last thirty boxes. We can do that easy before next weekend."

Everybody reverted back to not talking. That was okay. I knew Ashton didn't need to be pushed right now. He was hurting and he had the right to feel hurt. I'd wait until later to talk to him. I'd give him a phone call tonight. Although I wasn't exactly sure what it was that I was going to say when I did call him.

The phone kept ringing—four...five...and there was still no answer. I guessed nobody was home. Maybe that was better anyway because I still hadn't figured out what I was going to say.

There was a "click" and an answering machine came to life.

"We're not home," said a woman's voice. "At the beep please leave a message and we'll get back to you as soon as possible."

I hated leaving messages.

"Beep!"

I hesitated for a split second. Maybe I should just hang up. No, I better say something. "Um...hello...um...this is...um...Nick and—"

"Hey, Nick." It was Ashton.

"Hi. I didn't think anybody was in," I said.

"I'm home. I always listen for the machine. If it's not for me I just leave it. That way I don't have to take messages."

"That's smart."

"And safe. You don't have any big brothers, so you can't imagine how mad they get if you forget to tell them that some girl called."

"I know I get annoyed when somebody doesn't tell me that Kia called."

"This is a little more serious. These aren't girls who are friends but girlfriends. The worst, about two years ago, was when some girl called and asked for one of my brothers and I said he wasn't home because he was out on a date with his girlfriend."

"What's so bad about that?" I asked.

"What I didn't know was that he was out on a date with *one* of his girlfriends, and I was talking to another one who didn't know about the first."

I burst out laughing.

"Glad you think it's funny," he said. "My brother, my much bigger brother, didn't think it was funny at all. Speaking of funny, the message you started to leave was pretty funny."

"What was so funny about it?"

"Yeah, it sounded like you didn't remember your own name. 'Um...this is...this is...um... Nick.'"

"I don't like talking to machines," I explained. "So how you doing?"

"I'm doing just fine. Now."

"I thought you might need some time," I said.

"All I needed was time to make the right decision."

"Decision, what decision?" I asked. I didn't want him to make any decision.

"I'm quitting the team."

"You can't quit!" I exclaimed.

"Sure I can. Already decided. I'm not going back again."

"But you can't do that. You're a great player and the team needs you."

"Didn't you hear? The team doesn't need me because I'm not even part of the team."

"Of course you're part of the team!"

"No, I play me-ball not b-ball."

"He wasn't just saying that about you. Nobody was passing the ball."

"It doesn't matter. Haven't you figured it out? That coach wants me to quit. He doesn't want me on the team."

"Yes he does. If he didn't want you on the team, he wouldn't have picked you in the first place," I tried to explain.

"No, it's better for him if he picks me and then I quit. Then he can say it's my fault instead of the real reason," Ashton said.

"What do you mean, the real reason?" I asked.

"He's a racist."

"A racist! How can you say that?"

"Because he is. He's against me because I'm black."

"That's crazy!"

"Are you calling me crazy?" Ashton demanded.

"No, of course not. It's just that I know he isn't."

"Why else would he be so hard on me?" Ashton asked.

"He's hard on everybody. Last year at the start of the season he did some things to me that—"

"Did he ever leave you on the court all by yourself?" Ashton asked, cutting me off.

"No, but he did other things."

"He did that to me because he's a racist."

"But it's not like you're the only black kid on the team. More than half the guys are black, and none of them think he's racist."

"Have you ever asked them?" Ashton asked.

"No. Have you?"

"No."

"Maybe you should talk to them. Ask them what they think, because I already know the answer. The only color that matters to Coach is the color of your uniform. If you're wearing orange you're family. Couldn't you just stay with the team a little bit longer? Give it a chance. We're getting our new uniforms next week." I thought if I could get him to hang around a bit longer he might decide not to quit the team. "You've almost raised all the money. At least if you walked away then you'd have the uniform."

"If I walked away, do you think I'd even want one of the uniforms? They are probably the ugliest uniforms in the world!"

"They're not that bad."

"Bright orange?" he asked. "You look like either a traffic pylon or a basketball."

I didn't care if they were bright orange. I was proud of my uniform. It meant something to me. Something important.

"Could you at least talk to Coach about what you're thinking and that you want to quit the team?"

"I don't want to talk to him and that's why I didn't answer the phone when he called tonight."

"He called you?"

"Twice."

"And?" I asked.

"And he left two messages on the answering machine. Like I said, I didn't want to talk to him."

"And what did he say...you know...in the messages?" I asked.

"Something about wanting to talk. I didn't really listen. I just erased them from the machine."

"So you're not going to call him?"

"I'm not calling anybody, I'm not talking to anybody. I'm surprised I even picked up the phone to talk to you."

"Why wouldn't you talk to me?"

"I don't know. Maybe the reason you're defending him is because he's not the only one who's a racist."

"You think I'm a racist?" I exclaimed, unable to believe what he'd just said.

"You could be."

"Come on, Ashton, that's not fair. It's not like I ever did anything or said anything tha...hello...hello..." There was a dial tone. He'd hung up on me! What should I do now? Should I call him back? What was the point in that? He probably wouldn't even pick up the phone. I put the phone back in the cradle and then picked it up again. There was somebody I should call.

10

"Hi, L.B., is your Dad home?" I asked.

"Yep, he's right here. He said he thought he'd hear from you tonight."

"He did?"

"Yeah, hold on and I'll get him."

There was silence as he put down the phone. How did Coach know I was going to call him tonight?

"Hello, Nick."

"Hi, Coach."

"So are you calling to tell me that I'm being too hard on Ashton and that I have to back off?"

"Well..."

"Because that's what my son told me on the ride home after practice. Do you agree?"

I didn't answer.

"It's okay. I'm asking and I want an answer. An honest answer."

"Yeah."

"I think you and my son are right," Coach said. "You know how I sometimes take this stuff too seriously."

"For sure."

"But you'll notice I've been keeping my temper. I just have to keep in mind that you're all good basketball players but you're still just ten year olds, not college players."

This was going to be a lot easier than I thought.

"Ashton's a very talented player," Coach said.

"Very talented," I agreed.

"He probably has the most skills of anybody on our entire team."

I wasn't sure I was willing to go that far, but he was really good.

"The problem is I have to get him to realize that we're not playing run-and-gun street ball. If he doesn't learn that, he won't be able to develop as a player," Coach said.

But he also won't develop as a player if he quits the team, I thought, but kept my mouth shut.

"The kid has real potential. He could go somewhere. Basketball could be his ticket to university even."

"You think he's that good?" I asked.

"I think he could be that good."

"Maybe you should tell Ashton that," I suggested.

"The problem is, if I tell him, it's going to go straight to his head and he's going to play less like he needs to play and more like he's already playing."

"That makes sense, but you have to say something to him."

"I've tried to talk to him. I've left a couple of messages on the answering machine, but nobody's called me back yet. I'll talk to him at the next practice. It might even be better to do it face-to-face."

"Maybe it would be better," I said. Of course what I didn't say was that he wouldn't have that chance because Ashton wasn't coming to any more practices.

There was something I wanted to ask, something I needed to ask him. I didn't believe it for a minute—what Ashton had said—but I needed to know.

"Do you know what makes this even more difficult?" Coach said.

"What?" I asked.

"This is going to sound stupid," Coach said.

"What?"

"It would be different if I was black."

"If you were black? What do you mean?" I asked.

"Or Ashton was white. Sometimes when the player is black and the coach is white—or the other way around—these things get tied up into issues around black and white. I just hope that doesn't happen. I'd hate to think that Ashton thought I was being hard on him because he's black."

I didn't know what to say. All I knew was that Coach had gone exactly where I was planning on going myself. Maybe it wasn't just Kia who could read my mind.

"You know me, Nick. I'm hard on every-body."

I laughed. "I know, Coach." And I did know it. What I didn't say was that other people—Ashton—did have some ideas it was about race. Race...what a stupid thing to call it. My mother had once said to me that there really was only one race—the human race—and I agreed.

"Thanks for calling, Nick. I hope Ashton knows how lucky he is."

"Lucky?"

"Yeah. He's lucky he has a friend like you sticking up for him. See you Tuesday."

11

Slowly, hesitantly, we walked. The sidewalk was narrow. The street itself seemed narrow. Maybe that was just because the buildings rose up so high on all sides of us.

"This maybe wasn't such a good idea," I said.

"Not a good idea?" Kia asked. "It was your idea."

"I know it was my idea. That doesn't mean it was a good idea. I can admit when I'm wrong," I said. "Something some people could learn from."

"Never having been wrong, it's hard for me to understand," Kia replied.

"Right. Do you think we should just go home?"

"I didn't walk halfway across town to go home without trying. We're here, so let's just do it," Kia said.

"But if he wouldn't take our phone calls, how do we even know that he'll answer the door when we call on him?"

"We don't...and why didn't you think of that before we walked all this way? And why did we have to bring the carton of chocolate-covered almonds with us?"

"I was thinking that we could get Ashton to go out with us and finish selling the remaining thirty-three boxes. Then he'd have all his money for the registration and he might be more willing to play," I explained.

"But you said it wasn't about the money. It was about Coach."

"I know, but anything extra on our side wouldn't hurt," I said.

"I can't even imagine him thinking that Coach was being hard on him because he's black. Coach is practically color-blind— except for the color of the uniforms."

"That's what we have to explain to him.

That's what we have to convince him. That is if he'll even talk to us."

"He better talk to us after we came all this way."

"I just hope you're—"

"Look!" Kia exclaimed, cutting me off. "There are the basketball courts Ashton always talks about."

Squished in between two of the buildings sat a large paved area that held two—no, three—courts. There was action on every court. It looked like there were three different games going on. I would have liked to just go over and watch the games. I loved watching basketball almost as much as I loved playing it.

"That's where Ashton plays, I bet," Kia said.

"No bet. He told me the courts were right beside his building."

"Do you think that he might be there now?" Kia asked.

"I don't see him, but we have to pass right by anyway."

As we got close to the fence I tried to find Ashton. I couldn't see him. What I did see were people running up and down the courts. And, of course, there were the sounds: balls bouncing, sneakers squeaking, yelling, grunting, kids calling out for the pass.

I stopped walking, grabbed the fence and stared. They were all older than us—mostly teenagers and some guys who were like grown-up men. In the little snapshots of play that I was seeing it seemed like these guys were playing some serious ball: fancy dribbling, no-look passes and then an alley-oop that turned into a thunderous dunk! I yelled out my approval, joining the chorus of dozens of other people doing the same thing.

"Did you see that?" Kia exclaimed.

"That was amazing! Ashton said that there are games out here almost twenty-four/seven."

"That's how people get to be so good. That's how Ashton got so good," Kia said. "And speaking of Ashton, there he is!"

Ashton was sitting on his basketball on the sidelines of a game. The guys on the court were all older and bigger, and it was pretty clear that he wasn't waiting to play with them. He was just watching. I knew I could watch these guys play for hours.

"Ashton!" Kia yelled out and waved. Ashton and a half-dozen other guys all turned in our direction. Ashton didn't respond, although I didn't know how he could avoid seeing us.

"Ashton!" Kia yelled again.

He got up off his ball, picked it up and tucked it under his arm. He started to circle around the court to come over to the fence. It looked like he was deliberately moving slow... swaggering...trying to be cool.

"What are you guys doing here?" he asked. His tone of voice wasn't friendly and he wasn't smiling.

"We were in the neighborhood," Kia said.

"This neighborhood?"

"Actually we're in this neighborhood because we came to see you," I said.

"Why do you want to see me?"

I held up the box of chocolates. "We still have thirty-three more boxes of almonds to sell, remember?"

"Remember? Don't you remember the conversation we had last night? I'm gone. Done. Through. Finished."

"Okay, if you don't want to sell almonds, how about if we play some ball?" I asked.

"Here?"

"Of course here."

"You can't play here," Ashton said.

"Why not? Do you have to live here to play on this court?" Kia asked.

"Nope, anybody who can play can play here," he said.

"We can play. We've played rep ball for years," Kia said.

"I'm not talking rep ball. I'm talking real ball, street ball," Ashton replied.

"It's all real ball. Just different ball, and a good player, a real good player, can play all the different styles there are. Maybe you're not as good as you think you are and that's why rep ball is so hard for you," Kia said.

Ashton didn't answer, although I saw his expression harden. Only Kia could say something like that and get away with it.

"You'd be better to play on your driveway, anyway," Ashton said. "Here I have to wait until it's my turn before I can play."

"And is your turn coming up soon?" Kia asked.

"Soon. As soon as those guys are finished their game I can play. Matter of fact, those guys aren't even supposed to be playing there. The near court is just for kids under twelve."

"Those guys are a lot older than twelve," I said.

"A lot older. Some of them are practically senior citizens. There are guys there who are like twenty-five years old."

"Maybe somebody should tell them to get off," Kia said.

"Yeah, like they're really going to listen to me," Ashton said. "Do one of you want to try to kick them off?"

"Not me," I said.

"Me neither," Kia agreed.

"Then let's just watch them for now."

"That works for me. These guys look like they really know how to play," I said.

We followed Ashton along the fence until there was a hole. Then we ducked down and climbed through the opening.

"These guys are amazing," Kia said.

"A couple are okay," he said.

"Just okay?" I asked. "Did you see that dunk that one guy just made?"

"I saw. That looked good. Most of these guys are long on style, but there's nobody out there who can shoot from the outside."

I really hadn't noticed, but now that he'd mentioned it I realized that what he said was true. Every point I'd seen had been made from in the paint. Strangely, that was also the way Ashton played.

"We could make some real money if we brought that little white guy up here, you know, the one who can shoot," Ashton said.

"You mean Mark," I said.

"Yeah, that little Markie guy. We could set these guys up because every one of them figures they can shoot, but none of them can put the ball up the way that little Markie can."

"Do you think Mark can really outshoot these guys?" Kia asked.

"Easy."

"And he could win money off them?" Kia asked.

"No question." Ashton paused. "Course winning the money and walking away with it are two different things. Nobody would be real pleased if they lost to some little white kid."

Almost on cue a player, the player who had made the thunderous dunk, pulled up and took a jumper. It clanged off the rim and bounced over the top of the backboard and out of play.

"Whoa!" Ashton yelled loudly. "I've never seen a brick bounce that high before!"

Everybody on the court began to laugh. That is, everybody except the guy who'd tossed up the shot. He gave Ashton a scowl that would have peeled paint off a wall. I took a half step away from Ashton to escape the glare. The guy was big—bigger than anybody else out there—and that was saying a lot because there were a whole lot of big guys. He had a shaved head and a large tattoo on his arm and he looked mean. If I saw him on the street I'd be afraid. Heck, I *was* on the street and I was afraid.

"Were you trying to make it bounce like that?" Ashton yelled out as the guy stared at him. "Was that some sort of trick shot or something?"

"You should learn to shut up, Ashtray," the guy snarled.

"And you should learn how to shoot!" Ashton snapped back.

"What are you doing?" Kia hissed.

"Nothing, just explaining to this big gorilla that he needs to practice shooting rather than styling!"

The guy turned up the intensity of his glare but didn't say anything.

"Okay, next basket wins!" somebody yelled out.

The big guy trotted to his end of the court but kept an angry eye on Ashton as he ran back.

"Are you trying to get yourself killed?" I asked.

"From him? I'm not scared of him."

"If you're not, you're stupid," I said.

"You calling me stupid again?" Ashton demanded. He swung around and glared at me with a stare almost as intense as the one that had just been aimed at him.

"Of course he's calling you stupid," Kia said, stepping in between us. "And you have to be pretty stupid to pick a fight with a guy that big."

"I told you, he doesn't scare me. Matter of fact, none of the guys on this court scare me. Come on, you little babies!" Ashton yelled out. "Can't one of you make a basket so we can play?"

I couldn't believe what he was saying. Bad enough that he was insulting the biggest guy on the court, but now he was taunting everybody on the court. Did Ashton have a death wish, and more importantly, would Kia and I be included in that wish?

Thank goodness the players were all so intent on the game that they didn't seem to notice what he'd yelled at them. The players moved up the court again without anybody scoring. It suddenly seemed like everybody was interested in playing defense. There was

a steal at one end and then a blocked shot—
it was trapped against the glass—and then
another steal. It looked like the defenses on
both teams had collapsed into the paint,
stopping anybody from driving and daring
them to put up a shot.

"Give it to the big baboon!" Ashton yelled.

"Shut up, Ashcan," the guy threatened as
he ran back to get on defense.

"You should focus on the game and not on
the fans!" Ashton screamed after him.

"Ashton, you really shouldn't be bugging
him," I hissed. "He could kill you...he could
kill all of us."

"You afraid of him because he's black and
you think all black guys carry weapons or
something?" Ashton demanded.

I snorted. "I'm afraid of him because he's so
big he doesn't need any weapons to kill us."

"He's big, but that doesn't mean he's tough.
He's just a pussycat."

"A tiger is a type of pussycat, but I'm not
messing with one of those whether they're
orange, black, white or green."

"Look, he has the ball!"

The big guy grabbed a rebound and started up the court. He moved like a rocket and it was clear that nobody was going to beat him to the basket and—he pulled up and the members of the other team scrambled past him, blocking him from driving. Why did he do that?

He looked over at Ashton, smiled and then turned back to face the net. He was way outside the three-point line, but it looked like he was going to shoot. He put up a long, long ball. It spun ever so slightly with backspin as it sailed through the air and down and swooshed right through the basket, nothing but net!

His teammates all yelled and screamed and then rushed over and mobbed him with high fives, back slaps and a couple of chest slams.

The big guy looked over at us. He had a big, goofy smirk on his face.

"Talk about a lucky shot!" Ashton yelled out. "Were you even aiming for the basket or was that like a really, really bad pass that just went in by accident?"

I shuddered at his words as the big guy's smirk changed to a scowl and he started walking toward us. "I told you to shut up, you little Ashtray!" he growled.

"Who's going to make me shut up?" Ashton demanded.

If that wasn't the stupidest question I ever heard in my whole life, I didn't know what was.

As the guy came forward, both Kia and I backed a few steps away from Ashton. I had to fight the urge to simply turn and run for the hole in the fence and not stop running until I was inside my house...inside my house, with the door locked, hiding under the bed. Why had we even come here and whose stupid idea was it in the first...oh, yeah, it was my stupid idea.

Ashton didn't budge even a half inch as the guy came right up to him, towering over his head. He just stood there, his hands on his hips, glaring back at the guy. This was either the bravest or dumbest thing I'd ever seen. Possibly both.

"Do you know what I'm going to do to you?" the guy asked ominously.

136

"I'd like to see you try to do something," Ashton replied.

Like lightning the guy reached out, grabbed Ashton, lifted him up off the ground and—

"You leave him alone!" Kia screamed.

The expression on the face of the guy registered the shock I was feeling.

"Put him down this minute!" she demanded.

The guy chuckled but didn't release his hold on Ashton, whose feet dangled a good foot off the ground.

"I said put him down!" Kia yelled.

He dropped Ashton to the ground. "What if I pick you up instead?" the guy asked.

"Leave her alone!" I yelled as I stepped forward, putting myself between Kia and the guy.

He now looked doubly shocked. "Whoa, it's like a gang. A gang of little, tiny, white people."

The whole group that had been on the court was now standing around us, watching, grinning, laughing.

"You leave them alone!" Ashton yelled and pushed the guy—who didn't even budge as Ashton bounced against him.

"Leave all of us alone!" Kia repeated.

He looked down at Ashton and then cast a hard look at Kia and me.

"I wasn't planning on doing anything to the two of you," he said. "But I was planning on doing something to him." He pointed at Ashton. "And nobody, and I mean *nobody*, is gonna stop me."

He reached out and grabbed Ashton again, lifted him up and kissed him on the cheek!

"Don't do that, you big goof!" Ashton yelled.

He put Ashton down, and Ashton wiped his cheek with the back of his hand.

"What's wrong with me giving my baby brother a real big hug and a little kiss?"

"Your brother?" Kia and I echoed.

"Yeah, my brother."

The big guy lifted Ashton up again, this time even higher, and planted a big, noisy kiss on his forehead.

12

"You're his brother?" I asked, not believing what I'd just heard.

"His big brother. His biggest brother."

"I didn't know. We didn't know," Kia said.

"I'm not surprised. I'm so much better looking than Ashton that we don't even look like brothers."

"Shut up, Jamal!" Ashton snapped.

"Who's gonna make me shut up?"

"Me!" Ashton rushed at his brother, swinging and kicking and practically spitting. Jamal swept him off his feet, spun him upside down and held him up by his legs!

"Let me go!" Ashton screamed.

"If I let you go, you'll fall on your head and that could damage the pavement."

"Let me go!"

Jamal continued to hold him with one hand and began tickling him on the stomach. Ashton stopped screaming and began laughing and shaking and squirming, trying desperately to get away.

"Stop...stop...tickling me!" he yelled between the laughter.

"What's the magic word?" Jamal demanded.

"Stop tickling me...or...or I'm going to pee!"

"Not exactly the magic word I was looking for, but good enough to get you down."

He stopped tickling Ashton, flipped him back around and dropped him on his feet once again.

"You know, even Ashton wouldn't be stupid enough to pick a fight with somebody my size. Although to be honest I wouldn't put it past him. He's got himself in some strange situations over the years because sometimes his mouth starts moving way before his brain is in full gear and he says the dumbest things."

"Shut up, Jamal!"

"Who's gonna make...okay, we've already done this. So are you going to introduce me to your friends or are you going to be rude as well as stupid?"

"Shut up...fine," Ashton said. "Okay, this is Kia and this is Nick."

Jamal reached out and shook hands with Kia and then offered his hand to me. My hand practically disappeared into his huge mitt.

"Nice to meet you both. Do you two live around here?"

Ashton started laughing. "Come on, Jamal, look at them."

"I am looking at them. Do you have a point or are you just running off at the mouth again, baby brother?"

"Do they look like they live around here?"

"I don't see why they couldn't."

"They're white," Ashton said.

"Oh, my goodness!" Jamal said, sounding shocked. He bent down so he was at our level and looked directly at me, eye to eye. "Do you know that? Do you two know that you're white?"

I didn't know what to say or how to answer that. I giggled nervously.

"You're a real funny guy," Ashton said. "Real funny."

"Funny is good. Stupid isn't. So they're white. Big deal. You make it sound like there aren't any white people in this neighborhood. But if I'm not mistaken, your friend Brian from two floors below us is white, isn't he? And if you look around, aren't there at least half a dozen white guys here on the courts?"

"But there aren't many white people in the complex," Ashton said.

"Not many, but some," Jamal said. "To say there are no white people living here is just wrong, and I don't know why you'd even say that. There are probably the same number of white people living here as there are blacks who live in my neighborhood."

"Isn't this your neighborhood?" I asked.

"I guess in some ways it will always be my neighborhood because I grew up right here, but I haven't lived here since I graduated from college. My wife and I have a house over on the west side, close to my school."

"But if you've graduated from college, why do you still have to go to school?" Kia asked.

"It's important the teacher shows up or things tend not to get done."

"You're a teacher?" I asked.

"Both me and my wife. Emma teaches grade six and I'm a grade three teacher."

"Grade three!" I exclaimed.

"Yeah, grade three. Is there something wrong with me teaching grade three kids?" he asked.

"No, of course not. It just seems like you're so big and they're so small," I tried to explain.

"Tiny. I've got a couple of kids in my class who are smaller than the lunch I pack. Good kids though. My wife and I both love going to school every day. Of course she'll be taking some time off soon. We're expecting our first and second child."

"First and second?" Kia asked.

"We're pregnant with twins," he explained.

"We?" Ashton asked, sounding shocked. "Last time I checked, your wife was the one who was pregnant. Although," Ashton said, reaching out and patting his brother on the stomach, "it does look like you could be somewhere around six months pregnant yourself."

Both Kia and I started laughing and Jamal smiled. That smile was much nicer than his scowl and a lot less scary.

"I am putting on a little bit of weight since I haven't been playing ball as much," he admitted.

"A little weight? Watching you running the court is sort of like watching one of those super-slow-motion replays on television." Ashton began pretending he was dribbling a ball in slow motion.

"There's still one thing I don't understand," Jamal said. "You two seem like nice kids, so why are you hanging around with my brother? Couldn't you find somebody better to be your friend?"

"No," Kia protested. "We like Ashton a lot."

"You must be good friends," Jamal said. "Good enough to try to step between him and me. You two didn't know we were brothers when you tried to stop me. That took guts." Jamal turned to Ashton. "You got yourself a couple of good friends here. If they're not from the neighborhood, where did you three meet?"

"On my driveway," I said. "We invited Ashton to play basketball with us."

"So you two are players."

"Good players," Ashton said. "They play on the Mississauga Magic rep team."

"The team you're on," Jamal said.

"The team that I *was* on," Ashton corrected him.

"Was? Why aren't you still on the team?" Jamal asked.

"Lots of reasons."

"I've got time. Explain to me the lots of reasons you're not on the team," Jamal said.

"That would take too much time," Ashton said. "I just came here to play some basketball." Ashton turned and started to walk away

146

when Jamal reached over, picked him up off the ground and spun him around so he faced us again. For a split second it was like watching a cartoon as Ashton's legs continued to walk while he was suspended in mid-air.

"What are you doing?" Ashton demanded.

"Not letting you walk away." He dropped Ashton back to the ground. "Now explain to me why you're not playing for that team."

Ashton stuck out his jaw and puffed out his chest. He had a look that said "Just try to make me talk."

"First it was because of the money," I said, jumping in.

"What money?" Jamal asked.

"The registration fees to play rep ball," I explained.

"How much is it?" Jamal asked.

"Registration is three hundred and fifty dollars," Kia said.

"Three hundred and fifty dollars! That's a lot of money, but maybe I can help pay for it."

"I can't take your money," Ashton said. "You've got a wife and a house and kids on the way. You gotta take care of your family."

"And who do you think you are if you're not my family?"

"But that's all taken care of anyway," I said.

"It is?" Jamal asked.

"All except the last thirty-three dollars."

"Where did you get the rest of the money?" Jamal asked. "The three hundred and seventeen dollars."

"Selling chocolate-covered almonds," Ashton said.

"Like these," I said, holding up the box. "Every box sold is one dollar toward the registration fee."

"So you sold three hundred and seventeen boxes of almonds?" Jamal asked.

Ashton nodded. "Me and Nick and Kia. They helped me."

"You two helped him sell all those almonds?" Jamal asked.

"It wasn't hard," Kia said. "It only took us three nights...plus a day."

"And now we just have to sell the boxes that are in this carton—thirty-three more—and the whole registration is paid for."

"Tell you what. I love chocolate-covered almonds. I'll buy the last thirty-three boxes," Jamal said.

"No you won't!" Ashton protested.

"Yes, I will," Jamal said. "And I don't see how you can stop me."

"Fine, go ahead and buy them. I'm still not going to play."

"Why not?" Jamal asked.

"Because I don't want to."

"You don't want to play basketball?" Jamal asked like he couldn't believe his ears.

"I don't want to play basketball with them."

"With Kia and Nick?"

"No, with the rep team."

"But you said Kia and Nick are on the rep team," Jamal said.

"Yeah, but it's not them I don't want to play with."

"There are other kids on the team who you don't want to play with?"

"No, the other kids are okay."

"Then who exactly is it that you don't want to play with?"

"I don't want to play with that coach."

"What's wrong with the coach?" Jamal asked.

"He treats me bad because I'm black."

"He does what?" Jamal asked, suddenly looking very serious.

"He's a racist."

"That's not true!" Kia exclaimed.

"Are you saying he doesn't treat me bad?" Ashton demanded.

"Not bad. Tough. He's tough on everybody."

"Not as tough as he is on me," Ashton said.

"Maybe that's because he doesn't need to be as tough on everybody else as he is on you because everybody else actually listens to what he says!" Kia snapped.

"I listen," Ashton said.

"Well, maybe you should do more than listen and actually do what he tells you!" she scolded him.

"I don't need to hear this!"

Ashton started to walk away once more and again his brother stopped him. "Stay," he said. "Wait and listen."

Jamal looked at Kia and then at me. "What my brother is saying, if it's true, is very serious. Racism is a terrible thing."

"But he's not a racist!" I said.

"Maybe he isn't. Maybe he is. Why do you think my brother is wrong about your coach?" Jamal asked.

"Well, for one thing, half the kids on the team are black," I said.

"Yeah, so what? Maybe he treats them badly too."

"He treats everybody the same. Everybody. Black or white."

"He's not harder on my brother than the other kids?" Jamal asked.

"Well...he is pretty tough on Ashton," I admitted.

"Tougher than on he is on the other kids— white and black?"

"Maybe harder than everybody else."

"And is it like Kia suggested, because my baby brother doesn't listen?" Jamal asked.

"That and because of what he thinks of Ashton."

"What does he think?" Jamal asked.

"Yeah, I'd like to know that too," Ashton said.

I was in a bind. I'd brought the subject up in the first place, but could I really say what Coach had said to me? Would that be like blabbing? But then, what choice did I have now?

"Coach said he's been hard on Ashton because he thinks he has such potential. He thinks he could play at college."

"He said that?" Ashton asked.

I nodded. "He also said to me that he tried to call you because he thought he had been too rough on you and he wanted to apologize."

"Is that why he called?" Ashton asked.

"He said he left two messages on your machine and you didn't return his calls."

"Actually he left four messages. Two yesterday and two today. Wow, just think... he thinks I could play at college, like my brother."

"You played college ball?" Kia asked Jamal.

"Four years. Got an education from playing ball. Met my wife there."

"That's fantastic," I said.

"Of course, I always figured I'd be playing college ball on my way to playing professional ball. That just didn't work out...not that I'm unhappy about how things did work out."

"Who knows, maybe I could be the one in the family to make it to the NBA," Ashton said.

"Don't get all caught up in that," Jamal said. "You're good, but just because some coach thinks you can play college doesn't make it true. And just because you can play at college doesn't mean you can make the next step. This coach might not even know what he's talking about."

"But Coach would know," I said. "He really knows what he's talking about. He used to play at college. He even played for a couple of seasons in the NBA."

"He played in the NBA?" Jamal asked. He sounded surprised and impressed. "What's this guy's name?"

"It's Barkley," Ashton said.

"Len Barkley?" Jamal asked.

"I don't know what his first name is," Ashton said.

"It is Len," I confirmed. "Do you know him?"

"Of course I know him. My college coach used to be a teammate of Len Barkley when they played in college. He told us that he was one of the best college players of all time," Jamal said. "We didn't believe him until he brought us in footage. That guy could really play ball." Jamal turned to Ashton. "Didn't you know who your coach is?"

"I just thought he was some old guy with a bad leg," Ashton said.

"He's some old guy who was a great player," Jamal said.

"And he's a very, very good coach," I said. "We've improved a lot since he started coaching us. He really knows basketball."

"Do you think he knows basketball?" Jamal asked Ashton.

"I guess he knows something about basketball," he admitted.

"He knows lots about basketball," I said. "And he's already taught you a lot."

"He hasn't taught me anything," Ashton protested.

"He hasn't? Weren't you listening to what you were saying to your brother during the game?"

"You think he taught me how to insult my brother?" Ashton asked.

"Not insult, but the things you were yelling. Things about passing the ball and outside shooting and being a team player instead of just styling. Aren't those the same things Coach is always riding you about?"

Ashton didn't answer.

"You know, little brother, it's very rare to play for a coach who can help you become a better player. Believe me, I know. And it sounds like this guy could make you a better player. Somebody who could get you to college, where you could play some ball. Somebody who could help you go even farther...who knows?"

Ashton still didn't answer. I'd learned that meant he probably agreed but didn't know how to say it.

"Ashton, you can't waste an opportunity like this," Jamal said. "We both know you want to play ball. We both know you're a good player. And we all know you need somebody to ride you to be the most you can be. I would have given anything to have a coach like that when I was your age. Heck, I bet there's lots of things I could learn from him now that would make me a better coach myself."

"Coach?" I asked. "You want to coach?"

"I've volunteered to coach the senior team, the grade eight boys, at our school," he said. "And I've played a lot of ball, but I never coached anybody."

Kia and I exchanged a look. We both knew we were thinking exactly the same thing.

"You know, we're looking for an assistant coach on our team," I said.

"Me?" Jamal asked. "I don't know if I have the time to do that."

"You could always just come to one of the practices and watch and maybe talk to Coach Barkley," I suggested.

"Maybe you could come to this Tuesday's practice," Kia added. "It's from six-thirty to eight."

"I guess I could just come out and watch," he said.

"Maybe you could give Ashton a ride," I suggested. "But if it's out of your way, I can pick him up."

"Wait a second. Who even said I'm going?" Ashton protested.

"If I'm going, believe me, you're going!" Jamal exclaimed.

"Are you going?" Ashton asked.

"I'm going."

Ashton looked at his brother. "How about you pick me up around six?"

Jamal smiled. "You got it, little brother, you got it."

13

One of their players put up a long, desperate, three-point shot. They were so far down, with so little time left, that was all they could try to get back in the game.

The ball bounced off the rim and high into the air. As it started to drop down, Jordan leapt up and met it halfway. He came down with the ball and almost instantly passed it to Ashton. Kia, figuring that Jordan would get the rebound, had already taken off down the court. Her arms were up in the air, calling for the ball. All Ashton had to do was toss her a lob pass and she was free for an easy two points and—Ashton started dribbling, head down, not seeing her. The other team got back down court and Kia was now covered by at least two people.

"Time out!" Coach Barkley yelled. "Full time-out!"

The ref blew his whistle and the play stopped. As the players started to come in off the floor and the rest of us got up off the bench, I already knew what was going to be said. Maybe everybody knew.

"Ashton, didn't you see Kia?" Coach Barkley asked.

"Kia?" Ashton asked. Apparently not everybody knew.

"As in, your teammate. The one who was alone, completely open, standing under their net, waving her arms in the air—that Kia."

"If I had seen her, don't you think I would have passed?" Ashton asked.

"Now, that's an interesting question," Jamal said as he loomed over his brother. He looked over at Coach Barkley. "How about if we put in a sub and the assistant coach has a little chat with Ashton?"

"Good idea. A good teachable moment to help him understand what happened out there," Coach Barkley agreed.

Jamal had come out to that first practice—three weeks ago—and had been at every practice since then as our assistant coach. And if Ashton believed Coach Barkley had been riding him before, he must be starting to think that Jamal was his own personal jockey. Jamal was as hard on his brother as Coach was on L.B.—and that was saying a lot.

"Tristan go in for Ashton. D.J. go in for Kia," Coach Barkley called out.

"Why am I coming out?" Kia questioned.

"Because I'm the coach," Coach Barkley said. "Or do you want to discuss this at length? I'll even let you have the rest of the game on the bench to think about what you want to say."

"No, sir, you're the coach...no problem. I'll just go right over there and sit down and make sure I stay really quiet," she said and headed for the bench.

Jamal started to walk over toward Ashton. Neither looked particularly happy.

"Coach, Jamal," Coach Barkley called out, and Jamal turned around to face him. "Be gentle...okay?"

"I'll be as gentle as I can," he said.

The timekeeper signaled the end of the time-out. Tristan and D.J. ran over to the table to check in while the rest of us sat down. I took a seat beside Kia. I watched as the ball was put into play, but I wasn't nearly as interested in what was going to happen on the court as I was in what was going to take place behind our bench.

"This should be good," Kia said under her breath.

I turned my head, ever so slightly, so I could see Jamal walk his brother over to the side. I knew we were close enough to hear, especially if the conversation went the way I figured it might.

"You have to start looking up court," I overheard Jamal say.

"I look up the court."

"Then why didn't you see Kia?"

"Maybe I did see her...sort of," Ashton replied.

"I hope you didn't see her at all, because if you did see her open and still didn't pass, that makes you the worst kind of ball hog there is!"

Ashton didn't answer. I knew he hadn't seen Kia. His head was right down, watching his dribble, trying to avoid the other team's press.

"If you want to learn to play basketball, you have to learn to pass," Jamal said.

"I know how to play basketball!" Ashton snapped. "If you check the score sheet, you'll notice I have fourteen points!"

"Individual stats are for ball hogs and losers. What matters is the team. How many points you get means nothing unless your team is winning," Jamal said.

"What game are you watching?" Ashton questioned. "We're winning by almost thirty points!"

"And we'd be up by more if you'd hit the open man occasionally rather than trying to impress everybody. This isn't the street!" Jamal snapped.

"I know it isn't the street."

"I'm not sure you know anything some-times, but I'm going to help you learn something. I'm going to teach you exactly where you're going to be spending some time." Jamal pointed to the bench. "Sit. Maybe it'll give you a chance to think. Who knows, it might start a trend."

Ashton muttered something under his breath but walked over and plopped down beside me. He pulled up his jersey to wipe the sweat off his face and then took a big drink from his bottle.

"Have I thanked you yet?" Ashton asked.

"Thanked me for what?"

"For suggesting that my brother should become the assistant coach on this team."

"That's okay, I just figured he'd make a great coach and—"

"I was joking," Ashton said, cutting me off.

"You mean you wish he wasn't coaching us?" Kia asked.

"That's the general idea."

"But he's a great coach. He really knows

basketball and he and Coach Barkley get along well and—"

"And he rides me even harder than Coach Barkley ever did. I think they should put a saddle on me 'cause I feel like a horse—a horse with two people riding me."

"Come on, Ashton. Are you sure you're not just a little bit happy your brother is involved with our team?"

"Do I look happy?" Ashton questioned.

"Come on. Aren't you just a little bit happy about it?" Kia pressed.

"Well...maybe just a little, but only when he's giving somebody else a hard time. Why are they always so hard on me?"

"Do you really want me to give you an answer?" I asked.

"I guess not really."

"Nick! Ashton! Get ready to go in," Coach Barkley ordered.

I put down my water bottle and got up. Ashton got to his feet as well.

"Guys," Coach Jamal said, calling us over. "I want you two guys to run a little pick-and-roll action, okay?"

"Sure," I said and Ashton nodded.

"Nick, you set the pick on the left, high post, and Ashton, you make the pass when he rolls off for the net."

We walked over and stood by the scorer's table. The other team put up a basket that dropped, and Coach called for subs. The ref stopped the play.

"Jamie and D.J. out!" Coach Barkley yelled.

We jogged onto the court.

"Ashton, you put the ball in play," I said. "Pass it in to Tristan. Let him bring it up and we'll set."

Ashton tossed the ball to Tristan and he started to dribble. The other team was pressing, but Tristan broke through easily. He sent the ball up to Ashton and I set the pick for his man. My man jumped up to try to cut him off, and I spun around and headed for the net. Ashton lobbed a nice ball over their heads, right into my hands, and I put it up for two points!

Both of the coaches and most of our team jumped off the bench and began cheering. I

knew they weren't cheering my shot, but the pass that put me in for the shot. As I started back up court, I gave Ashton a pat on the back and a smile. He smiled back.

"Check out the bench," I said as we ran by. He looked over in time to see the two coaches exchanging a high five.

"You know," I said as we settled into our zone, "keep making passes like that and you could end up getting a lot of assists."

"That's right," he said. "Ten points and ten assists would get me a double double."

"It could mean a lot more than that," I said.

"What do you mean?"

"Look at the way the coaches and the other players reacted," I said.

"Yeah?"

"It gets you more court time. And it gets you respect. And it makes you something more important. It makes you part of a team."

"I am part of the team," Ashton said.

I wasn't going to argue. He was part of the team.

Other books by Eric Walters

Three on Three
Full Court Press
Hoop Crazy
Long Shot
Off Season
Road Trip

War of the Eagles
(Ruth Schwartz Award)

Caged Eagles
(UNESCO Honorable Mention)

Have you read *Off Season*?

*Book 6 in the Eric Walters'
basketball series*

Basketball season may be over, but Nick and Kia are about to experience the adventure of a lifetime when they visit Nick's cousin Ned during their summer vacation.

Though Ned is still more interested in bugs than basketball, his hoop skills are improving since he and his father built a court near their wilderness home. Nick and Kia are just beginning to appreciate the different life that Ned lives when disaster strikes.

Have you read *Hoop Crazy*?
Book 3 in the Eric Walters'
basketball series

Nick and Ned are cousins but about as different as two boys born on the same day can be. And they don't get along. Nick cares mostly about sports, and basketball is his passion. Ned is crazy about bugs and lives in a national park, three hours' drive from the nearest basketball court. As far as Nick is concerned, Ned is a nerd.

But when Nick and his pal Kia lose their teammates for the three-on-three hoop tournament they're entered in, they must quickly find a way to make Ned a part of the team. This turns out to be easier said than done.

Have you read *Long Shot*?

*Book 4 in the Eric Walters'
basketball series*

When Nick and Kia try out for the rep team they played for the previous year, they assume they will make the grade. That is, until they meet the new coach. Suddenly all their assumptions are thrown out the window. Coach Barkley, a former college star who missed out on a pro career due to injury, is a strict disciplinarian, and his aggressive coaching techniques are a new experience for the kids.

The new coach expects near perfection and does not deal well with anything less. When he matches them up against a team of older players and then refuses to accept their loss, the kids begin to wonder if they even want to make this team.

Long Shot is about the courage and leadership it takes to make difficult choices.

Have you read *Road Trip*?

*Book 5 in the Eric Walters'
basketball series*

Nick, Kia and their teammates are on the road, heading to an elite hoop tournament in the Midwest. Feeling outmatched by many of the high-profile teams that have been invited from all over the world, the kids are still looking forward to a good time—hanging out and swimming in the hotel pool between games. However, Coach Barkley, who played his college ball in the area and is still regarded as a hero, has other ideas. As usual, nothing but winning will be good enough for the coach.